AN EARLY DEATH

A RIGHT ROYAL COZY INVESTIGATION PREQUEL

HELEN GOLDEN

DREW BRADLEY PRESS

ALSO BY HELEN GOLDEN

A Right Royal Cozy Investigation Series

A Toast To Trouble (Novella)

Tick, Tock, Mystery Clock (Novelette)

Spruced Up For Murder

For Richer, For Deader

Not Mushroom For Death

An Early Death (Prequel)

Deadly New Year (Novelette)

A Dead Herring

I Spy With My Little Die

A Cocktail to Die For

Dying To Bake

A Death of Fresh Air

I Kill Always Love You

Murder Most Wilde

COPYRIGHT

This is a work of fiction. Names, characters, places, and incidents are the product of the author's imagination or used fictitiously. Any resemblance to actual persons, living or dead, events, or locales, is entirely coincidental.

ISBN (P) 978-1-915747-68-6

Edited by Marina Grout at Writing Evolution

Published by Drew Bradley Press

Cover design by Helen Drew-Bradley

First edition January 2023

DEDICATION

To my friend Steve.
Thank you for your friendship for all of these years. Thank you for listening to me when I try to fix things for you. Thank you for being my stately-home-visiting buddy. Thank you for being so supportive of my writing dreams. Sorry CID Steve didn't make it into this one. But one day he'll play a bigger role...

NOTE FROM THE AUTHOR

I am a British author and this book has been written using British English. So if you are from somewhere other than the UK, you may find some words spelt differently to how you would spell them. In most cases this is British English, not a spelling mistake. We also have different punctuation rules in the UK.

However if you find any other errors I would be grateful if you would please contact me helen@he lengoldenauthor.co.uk and let me know so I can correct them. Thank you.

For your reference I have included a list of characters in the order they appear and you can find this at the back of the book.

INTRODUCTION

An Early Death takes place fourteen years before *Spruced Up For Murder*, the first in the *A Right Royal Cozy Investigation* (ARRCI) series.

It covers the investigation into the death of James Wiltshire, the Earl of Rossex, and introduces Lady Beatrice, the Countess of Rossex (as a grieving widow), Perry Juke (as a nineteen-year-old tour guide), Simon Lattimore (working for Fenshire CID at the time) and Richard Fitzwilliam (only recently arrived at the Protection and Investigation (Royal) Services, PaIRS for short, and on secondment to the investigation team). At the time this book takes place, the king is Lady Beatrice's grandfather, His Royal Highness King Henry.

I have released this edition after *Not Mushroom*

For Death as I feel that is the best time to read this prequel. However, you can read it any time during the series, although I would recommend you read it before *I Spy With My Little Die* if possible.

Please note that this novel is intended to be read as part of the ARRCI series and not all elements of the mystery will be wrapped up neatly in this book.

1

10:30 PM, TUESDAY 3 JANUARY

James Wiltshire, the Earl of Rossex and heir to the Earldom of Durrland, raced his beloved Audi RS4 through the winding country roads of Fenshire, the headlights picking out an occasional glimpse of trees and hedgerows in the otherwise pitch darkness. He loved hearing her roaring engine and feeling the smooth, yet powerful pulling force. Even though he'd had her for just over six months, he'd yet to tire of the exhilarating drive, and as he didn't get to drive her very often, he was making the most of the quiet lanes to open her up.

As he approached a sharp left-hand bend, he eased his foot off the accelerator pedal — then slammed it on the brake as he rounded the corner.

In front of him were a dozen large black shapes blocking the road.

He clung to the steering wheel, about to turn it hard right to avoid them, when the herd of deer all pivoted and ran right, leaping into the woods.

Skidding to a halt, the car stopped just beyond where the deer had been standing only seconds before.

Blimey, that was close!

Slowly removing his foot from the brake, James let out the breath he'd been holding onto for the last three seconds. His heart pounded in his chest as he loosened his grip on the steering wheel and breathed in deeply to calm himself down. Once his heart rate returned to normal, he gently put the car into first gear and, at a much more sedate pace, continued on his way.

What was I thinking? He knew these twisty, winding roads well enough to be aware a driver had to be careful here, especially at night. Hadn't his wife Bea told him on several occasions to slow down on the local roads, knowing his tendency to speed?

"Darling, I don't want us to have to be pulled out of a ditch by a local farmer. Imagine what the press would say!" She had then laughed, so he'd known it had been a light-hearted admonishment, but he had also known she was right.

The deer could have been a broken-down car, and then where would I be now? Embedded in a tree, most likely.

Glancing at his watch, he turned left, following the sign for Francis-next-the-Sea — ten miles. He should make it home just before eleven and, if he was lucky, would be back in London by two-thirty in the morning at the latest. He could work with that; the unexpected change of plan, although inconvenient, would only result in a few hours of missed sleep.

He sighed. *Am I doing the right thing?*

Bea knew him too well not to have noticed how distracted he'd been lately while he'd wrestled with his problem. Her frequent enquires of, 'Are you all right, darling?', were becoming more persistent, and he knew it was only a matter of time before she would refuse to accept his response of, 'Yes, everything's fine,' and would confront him.

How would he tell her face to face he'd been deceiving her all this time? *She will be so upset and disappointed in me.* A shiver ran up his spine. He understood his decision to act was going to cause waves. *Is it too late to change my mind?*

He shook his head as he slowed down and

pulled up at the agreed meeting point. A woman stepped out of the cover of the trees as he brought the car to a gentle stop. As he opened the door, the cold air hit him.

No. It's too late now…

"Thank you," the woman whispered as he climbed out of the car. She wore a thick parka-type jacket, the hood obscuring much of her face. When she pulled the hood down and unbuttoned the coat, it was clear to James she'd been crying; her eyes were red and swollen, her cheeks wet and splotchy.

He opened the passenger door of the car. "Let me take those, and you get in. It's cold."

She shrugged off the dark-blue fur-lined anorak and handed it to him as he grabbed the wheeled suitcase she was pulling behind her. He deposited the items in the boot, and then walking around to the driver's side, he scanned the road behind and ahead of him before sliding into his seat. *Hopefully, no one has seen us.*

In the dark, the light from her mobile phone lit up the interior of the car. "Are you all right?" He stared down at her mobile phone screen but couldn't see what she was doing.

She looked up and smiled. "I am now." She followed his stare. "I'm letting a friend know I'm safe. She was worried about me waiting outside in the dark."

He nodded as he turned the ignition key. The Audi sprang to life. 'Goodbye, My Lover' blasted from the four-speaker sound system. *Hardly appropriate, you idiot!* "Sorry." James hastened to switch off the radio. "James Blunt gets everywhere these days."

He shrugged and smiled at her, but she was still concentrating on her phone. "Right," he said as he did a three-point turn and drove off in the direction he'd come from.

The woman sniffed, and he turned towards her. She wiped her face with the back of her hand. "I'm so sorry, James," she said, her blue eyes scanning his face. "I know this wasn't the arrangement, but I was so scared. Alex—" She stopped as she choked back the tears.

He leaned over and patted her arm. "It's okay. You're safe now." Trying to lighten the mood, he said, "What do you think of my baby?" He gestured around the interior. "I don't get to drive her much, so this is a real treat for me."

A boyish grin lit his face. She smiled slowly in

return. "It's very swish. I bet it can really move too."

"Just a bit," he said as he increased the pressure on the accelerator. "Let me show you what she can do." The car jerked forward as he selected the tiptronic option and accelerated through the gears.

"James, please be careful," the woman said, her voice holding a touch of anxiety. "These roads aren't made for speed."

James eased off the pedal and turned to smile at her. "Sorry, you're right. I get a bit carried away when the roads are quiet." He slowed the car down as they rounded the corner.

But it was too little, too late.

James saw a shape in the darkness ahead of them and hit the brakes hard. But this time, the object didn't disappear.

"Look out for the car!" the woman cried.

As he instinctively tugged the steering wheel sharply to the right to avoid it, a thought briefly crossed his mind. *What's a car doing in the middle of the road with no lights on?*

The Audi screeched as it went sailing off the tarmac, bouncing along the rough grass by the side of the road.

Oh heck!

There was a blood-curdling scream. It may have

been the woman, but then again, it may have been him as he fought to control the wheel.

But there was nothing he could do.

I'm so sorry, Bea!

The Audi plunged down the shallow embankment, rolling over once, twice. *Boom!* It eventually stopped when it ploughed into a two-hundred-year-old oak tree.

2

TWO WEEKS EARLIER. EVENING, SUNDAY 18 DECEMBER

Detective Sergeant Richard Fitzwilliam from the Protection and Investigation (Royal) Services regarded his wife across their dining table in bewilderment. *How did this happen? One minute, we're having a cosy chat about our day, and the next minute, I'm in trouble because I said the wrong thing. Again!*

Scraping her curly mid-length blonde hair into a tight ponytail, Amber Fitzwilliam glared at him as she wrapped a hair elastic around it with lightning speed. She crossed her arms and banged them down on the table in front of her, clearly waiting for his response.

"Look, I get you need a break from work, Amber," he said, trying to placate her. "So if you want to take time off, then that's fine with me." He smiled tentatively, hoping to sound like the supportive husband he wanted to be.

"Well, that's gracious of you," she sneered. "But you're missing the point!" She uncrossed her arms and grabbed her half-full wineglass. Taking a large glug of the still cool Chardonnay, she sighed. "I want to spend time with *you*, Rich, as well as have some time away from work."

"But I can't take three weeks off over Christmas and New Year. As the newbie, I'm expected to work over the holidays. Protecting the royal family isn't a part-time job." He was trying to keep the frustration out of his voice, but she was a police officer too. She knew how this worked. *Why is she giving me such a hard time?*

"Yes, yes, so you keep saying. But couldn't you at least ask? What harm can it do? You've been putting in stupid hours since you transferred to PaIRS, and apart from the week in June, which I had to beg you to take, you've not had any time off. They must owe you so many hours. Surely you can ask to take some of them now?"

"It's different in PaIRS, Amber. At City, you get to take your overtime in-lieu. We don't have the option of overtime. We simply do the job, however many hours it takes. And anyway, I've taken time off this year. I was off for your birthday, if you remember."

"That was in April, Rich. And before you say it, yes, you took a day off so we could have a long weekend in September with my family. Then you spent most of the Saturday on the phone with work and left early Sunday morning because someone had found something out that couldn't wait." She finished the wine in her glass and blew out a long breath. "It can't always be about work, Rich. You need to find a work-life balance. We need time for us." Her face, normally smooth and pretty, was distorted by the heavy frown on her forehead, making her look much older than her thirty-one years.

Fitzwilliam instinctively shook his head. Someone or other was always going on about work-life balance. *It's all a load of mumbo-jumbo if you ask me.* It might be important when you got older, but he was young, full of energy, and ambitious to get on. Why not prioritise work now so they *could* take more time off when they were established in their careers?

Husband and wife sat in silence for a few minutes. Neither of them looked at the other. Fitzwilliam sensed he should respond, maybe say sorry. *But I'm not sorry.* This was the reality of his job, and he didn't understand why she was making such a big deal about it.

When he and Amber had met four years ago, she'd been as ambitious as him. Their relationship had been supportive, and they'd enjoyed each other's successes. Fitzwilliam had been immensely proud of his wife when she'd received her promotion to sergeant six months before him. He'd even thrown a surprise celebration party for her.

When he'd become a sergeant, she'd initially been pleased for him too. They'd talked about the challenges of managing a team together, helping each other figure out the best way to handle various situations.

It had been when he'd been selected to move over to the prestigious Protection and Investigation (Royal) Services, PaIRS for short, that their relationship had changed, and the camaraderie had slowly disappeared.

Not long after, Amber had begun to complain about her job, moaning about the long hours and her 'useless' colleagues. She'd slowly become more and more resentful that she hadn't been finding the job satisfaction he had. Previously keen to get promoted, when he'd asked her when she was going to study for her inspector's exams, she'd surprised him by responding, "I'm not sure I will. The higher you reach, the more mess you have to deal with without support or resources to do the job properly."

It had seemed to him she'd lost her motivation. He'd suggested maybe a move would be good for her (there were dozens of special project teams in the City Police), but it had been met with a shrug and a, "Maybe". He'd even suggested she tried for PaIRS, but she'd simply laughed, saying, "A woman in PaIRS? I think your boss is the only one they allowed in, isn't she? I don't stand a chance." He'd argued that she should try anyway, pointing out that that was the way to get these things changed, but as far as he knew, she hadn't explored any of the options they'd discussed.

He, by contrast, had found his new job fascinating and had happily put in the extra hours. Lapping up the knowledge he'd been gaining and finding his place in the team, he'd enthusiastically shared with Amber how much he'd been thriving at work. He'd been disappointed when she'd stopped bothering to hide her disinterest anymore.

When he'd first accepted the job, she'd questioned him about why he'd opted to work within the intelligence team at PaIRS rather than join the more high-profile investigation and protection side of the organisation. He'd tried to make her understand he liked to make the connections and follow the trails. It was pro-active rather than re-active. *It's exciting.* But she hadn't understood his view.

He shook his head. *We seem to be heading in different directions these days.* Hopefully, it wasn't anything to worry about. *We'll figure it out.*

Amber sighed loudly. "Rich, we need this. We haven't spent any quality time together for ages, and I'm scared we're growing apart."

Fitzwilliam looked up at his wife. She had her head bowed, and a tear slowly ran down her cheek. *Oh no, what have I done?* He reached over and grabbed her hands. "I'm sorry, love. Believe it or not, I'm doing this for us. While I'm finding my feet, I need to show them I'm committed and working hard." He looked down at her hands in his. They were petite, like her. He lifted his gaze to her face. Reaching out, he brushed a tear from her cheek with his thumb. "Come on, bird, cheer up. We're good. We're strong. We can get through this. It will get easier, I promise." He gave her a tentative smile, and she smiled weakly back.

He loved how it always made her smile when he called her *bird*. Although he'd not lived in Leeds since he'd joined the Army at sixteen, he still used the term of endearment that had been prevalent during his childhood. Only when they were on their own, of course. It was hardly a politically correct word to use about one's spouse in public.

She raised her hand and gently stroked the stubble on his face. "Okay, bloke. I get this is a crucial time in your career. All I want to do is make sure there's an '*us*' left at the end of all this."

He nodded, and bending his head, he kissed the hand still resting on his face. For a minute, they sat there, enjoying the tender moment before she dropped her hand and rose.

"When I get into the office tomorrow, I'm going to book three weeks' leave starting on the twenty-third. Please try to get at least some of that period off too," she said as she rubbed her face.

"I'll see what I can do," he said, knowing deep down it was unlikely they would grant him any time off but not wishing to upset her further.

Heading to the kitchen area, her empty wineglass in her hand, she stopped and turned. "Thanks. But just so you know, I will do something without you if I must. I need this, Rich."

3

MEANWHILE. EVENING, SUNDAY 18 DECEMBER

Lady Beatrice, the Countess of Rossex, sighed as she sat down on the sofa in front of the coffee table in the drawing room of The Dower House on the Francis Court Estate. She felt as if someone had sucked the energy out of her. She glanced over at the carriage clock on the sideboard to her left. *I can't believe it's only nine-thirty.* It felt much later. *I can't go to bed this early, can I?*

"Are you all right, sweetheart?" Her husband followed her into the room and made himself comfortable in the armchair opposite. Penny, their black Labrador, settled by the side of the chair, and James rested his hand on the top of her head.

Bea smiled weakly. "Yes, I'm fine, just tired. It

was an early start this morning, and I think it's caught up with me."

"Ah, yes, your visit to the fish market in Carmouth. I forgot to ask you over dinner how it went."

"In one word — smelly!" *Oh, the stink!*

He laughed as his wife wrinkled her nose at the memory of it.

"In fact," she continued, "I was so nearly sick that I had to ask Rory to rush us through so I could get outside into the fresh air. I dread to think what they must have thought of me practically running to get out of the place." She laughed now, but at the time, she'd been embarrassed for bailing out on the people who had organised it so soon after her arrival. *But that smell...*

"Excuse me, your lordship, my lady, but will you be wanting coffee now?" Bea jumped. She hadn't heard Fraser enter the room through the door behind her.

"Yes, please, Fraser. Coffee would be great. Sweetheart, do you want anything else?"

"Actually, I think I'd prefer tea, please, Fraser. Earl grey if you have it. No milk."

"Yes, my lady." Fraser bowed and backed out of the room.

"Earl grey tea? That's an odd choice for this time of night."

"I know. I just fancied it." She shook her head; she normally loved coffee after her meal, but tonight it didn't appeal to her.

James rose from the armchair, Penny trotting behind him as she always did, ever since she'd been given to him as a present from his parents when he'd been in his late teens. He strolled over to the writing desk nestled along the wall to the left of the large French windows leading to the patio. The curtains had yet to be closed, and it was pitch-black outside. In the distance, Francis Court was lit up like a beacon on a hill.

Bea shuffled herself into a more comfortable position on the sofa, her back now in the corner and her left arm resting on a cushion. Stretching her long legs before her, she crossed them at the ankles. She studied her husband across the room. His tall lean frame was bent over the writing desk as he picked up some papers one by one, adding them to a new pile once he examined them. His fine brown hair fell over his face, and he brushed it out of his eyes. She smiled. *He's so handsome.* Except now there was a frown on his exposed forehead. *I wonder what he's looking for.*

"Are you looking for anything in particular, darling?" She had to raise her voice to reach him on the other side of the room.

He turned, the frown disappeared, and he smiled. "I'm looking for the notes I made when I was in Miami for the Olympic bid last month. I can't find them in my office, so I thought maybe I left them in here." He turned back and picked up the last piece of, as yet, unreviewed paper, glanced at it, then shook his head. "But it would appear not."

He sighed and walked back to resume his seat. Penny stretched out on the rug between him and the coffee table and closed her eyes. "Pen." He laughed gently. "Could you've found a more awkward place to lie?" The dog looked up at him, huffed, and slumped down again. She wasn't moving any more this evening. Still grinning, James shifted the chair further away so he could get his legs around the sleeping dog and returned his attention to his wife. "I'll have another look in the office in the morning. I must have missed them."

"Are they important?"

"Yes, I rather think they—"

Fraser's entrance with a trolley containing their hot drinks interrupted him. The butler stopped by the side of the coffee table and removed a silver tray with a coffee pot, a small silver milk jug, and a cup and saucer, and placed it in front of the earl. "Your coffee, my lord," he announced.

"Thank you, Fraser."

Fraser returned to the trolley and retrieved another smaller silver tray with a bone China teapot at its centre. "Your tea, my lady," he said as he placed it in front of her.

"Thank you, Fraser." She nodded at him, then grinned at her husband as Fraser turned his back on them and headed towards the French doors.

As she poured her tea and James his coffee, Fraser pulled the heavy lined curtains across the double windows, then moved over to the drinks cabinet on the right-hand side. He bent down, and opening the glass doors, he removed another silver tray, two cut glass tumblers, a small pair of silver tongs, and a decanter of whisky. Putting the tray in the middle of the sideboard, he arranged the decanter, tongs, and glasses on it. When he returned to the serving trolley, he picked up a small jug of water and an ice bucket. Carrying them to the drinks cabinet, he laid them on the tray next to the decanter, then walked back to where they were sitting. "Will that be all, my lord?"

James raised his eyebrows at his wife, who shook her head, a grin still playing on her lips.

I mustn't laugh.

James nodded. "Yes, thank you, Fraser. Good evening."

The butler bowed to them, and pushing his trolley, he left the room, closing the door behind him.

Bea snorted, no longer able to contain her amusement. "Why do we allow him to go through this rigmarole every evening? He could simply leave the trolley, and we could do it ourselves."

Also laughing, her husband said, "I know. But he likes to do it. A man of habit is our Mr Fraser, and I wouldn't want to disturb his routine."

He rose and made his way to the drinks cabinet. Glancing over his shoulder, he asked, "Do you want a whisky?"

"No, thank you, darling. I'll stick with my tea for the moment." Just the thought of alcohol made her feel nauseous.

He returned, drink in hand, and walked around Penny to sit back in the armchair.

"So tomorrow the plan is to leave at around nine to travel to London. I hoped to make it a bit later, but Rory is worried we may get delayed by Monday morning traffic. He thinks we need to give ourselves plenty of time. What do you think?" Lady Beatrice asked. Her husband was staring at the whisky glass in his hand and didn't respond. *What's wrong with him tonight?*

"James?"

He raised his head. "Sorry, sweetheart. I was miles away."

"Are you all right, darling? You seem a little distracted; I noticed it at dinner."

He leaned back in his chair and, sipping his whisky, said, "I'm sorry. I'm fine. Nothing to worry about. I just have a lot going on in my head at the moment."

Like what? Talk to me... "Can I help?"

"No, I don't think so, but I appreciate the offer."

Should I insist? This wasn't the first time in the last few weeks he'd drifted off into his own world. *Something is clearly bothering him.*

He placed his empty glass on the table and rose, making his way over to where she was sitting. "Actually, Bea, do you mind if I go back to my office and search for those notes?"

She scanned his face as he leaned over and kissed her forehead. *I wonder why these papers are so important?* She smiled up at him. A frown creased his otherwise smooth forehead. *He's obviously worried about it.* "That's fine. You go." She picked up her cup of tea and a copy of *Country Life* magazine. Sipping the perfumed brew, she watched Penny trundle off after her master.

Fifteen minutes later, feeling her eyes drooping,

she closed the magazine and stood. *It's no good. I really must go to bed.* Leaving the drawing room, she turned right along the wide tiled hallway, past the dining room, and paused as she heard James's voice coming from the study. *I thought he was looking for papers?* She glanced at her watch. Ten-thirty. *It's a bit late to be on the phone.* She crept forward towards the study door, which was slightly ajar.

"I need to see you," James said in an urgent voice. *Who's he talking to?* There was silence, presumably while the other person responded.

"All right." James sighed. "But no one must know about it."

Bea halted. *Know about what?*

"I'm worried—" He broke off suddenly. "What is it, Pen?" His voice moved towards the door. Penny must have sensed her presence.

"Hold on a sec," he said to the person at the other end of the line.

Bea frantically scanned the hallway. She couldn't be caught snooping on her husband. She bent down and dragged off her shoes, then rapidly tiptoed past the door and ducked around the corner just before the bottom of the stairs as she heard the door open. Flat against the wall, she held her breath, imagining James looking up and down the corridor.

"Sorry, yes, I'm fine." James's words echoed around the wood-panelled hallway. "So how soon can we…" His voice faded as he went back into the study, a click informing Bea he'd closed the door behind him.

She let out a long breath. *That was close!* She collapsed back against the wall and stared up at the grand sweeping staircase ahead of her. *What was that all about? Who does James have to see so desperately?* She pushed herself away from the wall and straightened up.

What is it about his trip to Miami the month before last that is worrying him so much?

She suppressed a yawn. She'd ask him in the morning. Right now, she needed her bed. Her shoes still in her hands, she crept out of the shadows and made her way quietly up the stairs.

4

EARLY MORNING, FRIDAY 23 DECEMBER

Fitzwilliam reached out for the two large suitcases his wife had just dragged down the hallway of their ground-floor flat.

"Are you finally leaving me?" He grinned as he grabbed them from her and carried them to the front door. Planting the cases down on the doormat, the laughter died in his throat when he turned and saw Amber's face.

She stood with her hands on her hips, a large scowl planted so firmly on it, only a pneumatic drill could remove it. "Is that a joke?" she snapped. "Because I'm not in a laughing mood, Rich."

He sighed and shrugged. *She appears to be having a complete sense of humour failure this week.* "Okay, sorry. I was trying to lighten the mood a bit."

"Well, don't bother," she griped as she stuck her head round the open kitchen door and snatched a set of keys from the key rack.

I know I should let it go, but she's being so unfair. He couldn't help himself. "I don't understand why you're still upset with me, Amber. I'll be with you on Boxing Day for the day, and all being well, I can take time off when everyone gets—"

She cut him off. "I'm still hacked off, Richard, because I don't think you even tried to get any time off over Christmas and New Year."

Richard? There was no doubt about the level of hacked off she was — she'd used his full name. She only did that when she was *really* upset with him.

"Of course I tried," he replied. "But I warned you, as the newbie, I'm expected to cover this time of year." *How many times do I have to repeat this before she gets it?*

"So how come Hayden Saunders got three weeks off to go mountain climbing in Mexico?" She yanked open the door of a built-in cupboard in the hall and grabbed a dark-green full-length puffa coat, slamming the door shut behind her.

Who? "Who the heck is Hayden Saunders?"

"He works for PaIRS, *and* he's been there less than a year. He's even more of a newbie than you are, but he still managed it!" She flung her coat on top of the two suitcases and turned to face him. Her blue eyes flashed as she glared at him.

I've no idea how he wangled that. Lucky so and so. Maybe his boss was more flexible, or someone had volunteered to cover for him... "Well, I don't know who he is, but he doesn't work in my area. Maybe it's different outside of Intelligence?" *It's not my fault!* He jerked his shoulders up in a violent shrug and stared right back at her.

"And." She seemly wasn't finished yet. "I know Freddie Stamp is on leave on Christmas Day *and* two other days over New Year. He's only been there for six months" —she threw her arms in the air— "and he *is* on your team!"

Rats! I didn't think she'd find out about that. "How on earth do you know that? Are you spying on me?"

Lowering her arms, she crossed them over her chest. Her shoulders sagged as if the fight had suddenly gone out of her. "He's the brother of one of the female officers in my team. It's a small world, Rich, you know that."

He should have known it would get out. *I*

should have told her before she found out through someone else. Now he was in the doghouse because he'd forgotten to ask for leave before Freddie had jumped in and requested the time off.

His wife sighed and turned away to pick up her coat. "I need to get going before the traffic gets heavy," she mumbled as she opened the door.

Fitzwilliam picked up her cases and followed her out to the car. He stowed them in the boot and went round to the open driver's door, where Amber was already buckling up her seat belt. *I don't want her to leave still upset with me.* He leaned towards her. "Amber, I'm sorry. I promise you I tried. Freddie got there before me, that's all."

She flipped down the sun visor to screen her eyes from the low early morning sun and shrugged. "I'll see you on Monday," she said as she switched on the engine. Smiling weakly at him, she pulled the door closed and drove down the hill, leaving him standing on the doorstep.

Rats!

Amber: *Yes, it was fun to chat last night. A coffee would be great. I'm on my way to Kent now, just stopped for the loo! How about tomorrow 10am at Chico's? x*

Dave: *Whoever invented Friends Reunited has my eternal gratitude! Sounds great. Really looking forward to it. Have a safe journey. See you tomorrow. x*

5

LUNCHTIME, FRIDAY 23 DECEMBER

"Are you sure you're all right, Bea? You look pale, and you've hardly eaten anything." Lady Sarah Rosdale tilted her head to one side and raised a well-sculpted eyebrow at her younger sister sitting opposite her.

"Yes, I'm fine." Bea picked up her fork and speared a spinach and ricotta stuffed tortellini dripping in sage butter before raising it to her mouth.

"Bea, come on, something is bothering you. What is it?" Sarah picked up a glass of water from in front of her on the enormous walnut table in the dining room at The Lodge and took a sip. Her eyes never left her sister's face.

Bea sighed. Sarah knew her too well to be fobbed off with a declaration that she was fine. She swallowed the pasta and placed her cutlery on her plate. "It's James."

Her sister, a strand of tagliatelle hanging off her fork and on its way to her mouth, stopped, her eyes widening. "James? What about James?"

"I don't know. But something's not right."

"Something like what?"

"I think it has to do with his trip to Miami back in October. Last week after dinner one evening, he couldn't settle because he mislaid some notes he'd made while he was there. Even though it was late, he went off to his study to look for them."

Sarah frowned. "I thought you had a no-work-after-dinner rule?"

Bea smiled wryly. "We do. But he looked so desperate when he asked if I'd mind if he went to look for them, that I couldn't say no."

"Did he find them?"

"I asked him the next day, and he said yes. But he still seems distracted and a bit distant."

Am I imagining it all? She herself had felt a bit out of sorts this last week or so. Was that making her super sensitive and seeing problems that weren't really there? But then there had been that call…

Sarah finished her mouthful, and placing her

fork down, she pushed her plate to one side. "There's more, isn't there?"

How does she do that?

"Later that same evening as I was going up to bed, I overheard him on the phone in the study. He was telling the person on the other end that he needed to see them. He sounded awfully keen."

"Do you know who he was talking to?"

Bea shook her head. "No. But it was quite late, gone ten-thirty. Then... well then, he said no one should know about it."

Sarah uncrossed her legs and leaned across the table towards her. "You don't think he's having an affair, do you?"

What!? Bea swayed backwards as if the wind had been knocked out of her. She grabbed the edge of the table, steadying herself. *How could she think that?* She glared at Sarah. "No. Of course not. How could you think that of James?"

Sarah leaned back, raising her hands defensively. "I thought that's where you were going with this. You know, mysterious late night calls arranging to meet someone in secret..." She tailed off and looked down at the table. "Sorry," she mumbled.

A cold shiver ran down Bea's spine. *She can't be right can she? Surely James wasn't arranging to meet another woman?* She closed her eyes, trying to recall the tone of his voice when she'd overheard him. No. He hadn't sounded like a desperate lover to her. He'd sounded concerned, like he'd needed help with something. And hadn't he said he was worried? She mentally shook herself. *What am I doing? I know my husband better than anyone. He would never betray me with someone else...*

Sarah coughed, and she opened her eyes. Their gazes met, and Sarah smiled. "Of course you're right. James isn't the sort." She reached over and took Bea's hand in hers. "And anyway, he adores you. I'm sure it's nothing to worry about," she said with conviction. "It's been a busy few months, and we're all tired. I bet after a good break over Christmas and New Year, he'll be feeling rested and back to normal. Okay?"

Bea let out a sigh of relief and smiled back at her sister as she squeezed her hand. *Of course, Sarah is right. It's most probably nothing more than a touch of end-of-year blues.* It would all be fine.

6

MIDDAY, SATURDAY 24 DECEMBER

The Society Page online article:

The Earl and Countess of Durrland Arrive at Francis Court in Fenshire

William and Joan Wiltshire, the Earl and Countess of Durrland, arrived at The Dower House in Fenshire this morning to celebrate Christmas with their only son James Wiltshire (24), the Earl of Rossex, and his wife Lady Beatrice (21). The seven-bedroom home is in the grounds of the twenty-five-thousand-acre family estate Francis Court, owned by Lady Beatrice's parents Charles Astley, the sixteenth Duke of Arnwall, and Her Royal Highness Princess Helen.

The Astley family has had a busy week leading up to Christmas. On Sunday, we reported the christening of Robert Louie Rosdale, HRH Princess Helen's first grandchild and son of Lady Sarah (24) and her husband John Rosdale (26), took place. The service, held at St Peter's Church, which is attached to the Astley family estate, was attended by their royal highnesses, King Henry and his wife Queen Mary, along with other members of the royal family. Robert, who was born in September, is the king and queen's first great-grandchild. Lady Sarah, her husband, and young son have recently moved into Francis Lodge, a seven-bedroom house built in 1695, in the grounds of Francis Court.

On Wednesday, the Earl and Countess of Rossex attended the wedding celebration of singer Erick Barber and his partner of seven years Ricardo Barry. Theirs was the third same-sex civil partnership registered in the United Kingdom on the day the civil partnership act came into force.

Yesterday, HRH Princess Helen's son Lord Frederick Astley (24), Earl of Tilling, accompanied the Prime Minister to Iraq for a surprise visit to British troops. The king's grandson is a serving officer in the Army.

The Astley family is expected to spend Boxing Day at nearby Fenn House, joining other members of the royal family for the traditional Boxing Day service at St Stephen's Church, followed by a lunch hosted by the king and queen. Their majesties are due to spend six weeks at Fenn House in Fenshire, as they do most years.

7

EVENING, SUNDAY 25 DECEMBER

"Well, I'm glad you've had a good day, Mum." Fitzwilliam said into his phone as he looked up at the towering building in front of his car, keen to keep the call short so he could get inside where it was warm and there was food waiting. The light streaming from the flats surrounding the car park in Dulwich where his sister and future brother-in-law lived created watery reflections in the puddles scattered around the tarmac from the earlier downpour. *No white Christmas again this year. Just a wet one.*

"I'm sorry I had to cancel on you and Elise at the last minute, but Dougie begged me to stay and help him with his mam. She's such a poor old soul, what with her arthritis and poor circulation. He can't manage her on his own."

Won't more like. And why would her mother's useless boyfriend even try when she was willing to take on all his responsibilities for him?

"And I'm glad I said yes as his brother rang up last night to say they had had their electric cut off." Fitzwilliam shook his head as she continued, "So Dougie invited him and his wife to stay here at my place with us until they can get the electricity key filled up. I've no idea what they would've done otherwise as there's no space in Dougie's tiny flat."

Fitzwilliam had to bite his tongue to stop himself from making a comment about Dougie and his scrounging relations.

His mother took a deep breath, then carried on. "I had to pop out to the late-night Spar shop to get extra food. Which is just as well as Dougie's eldest Tey was on the doorstep first thing this morning after his wife threw him out."

Unbelievable!

"So it's been a bit of a squash, but it's lovely for Dougie to have his family here."

He shook his head again. He wouldn't waste his breath telling his mother what he thought. Both he and his sister Elise had tried to warn her about that man, but their concerns had fallen on deaf ears.

"You don't understand him," she'd said. "He's a

softy under the brash, uncaring exterior," she'd promised. "And I love him."

Didn't she always? Every loser. Every waster. Every misunderstood sluggard she'd hooked up with was always 'the one'. Her prince charming.

Fitzwilliam sighed. "I hope you didn't spend the whole day cooking and looking after everyone, Mum. Did you get some time to sit down and relax?" He knew the answer before she opened her mouth to reply. *Am I as delusional as her, hoping every time it will be different?*

"Dougie took them all off to the pub at lunchtime so I could get dinner ready. So that was nice. I fed his mother early and got her all sorted, so she was back in front of the television for the King's Speech. They got back later than I expected, so I sat down and watched some of it with her."

They all take advantage of her, but what can I do? He'd talk to Elise again and see if she could persuade their mother to come down for a brief break in the New Year. He heard shouting in the background.

"Okay, son. I need to go as Dougie's mam needs putting to bed. Send my love to Elise." And with that, she was gone.

Fitzwilliam, a frown still creasing his forehead, put his phone in his jacket pocket, and reaching over to the passenger side of his car, he grabbed the carrier bag resting in the footwell. He opened the door and, avoiding the puddle he'd inadvertently parked next to, got out. Walking across the car park towards the entrance of the block of eight flats where his sister lived, he tried to shake off his annoyance, not wanting to let his mother's poor choices in life impact his ability to enjoy what he had left of Christmas Day.

"Thanks, sis, I've been looking forward to this all day." Fitzwilliam smiled at his sister Elise as she placed a plate in front of him containing three large thick slices of turkey breast and two huge Yorkshire puddings. *I'm so ready for this!*

"Help yourself to vegetables, stuffing, and gravy," Rhys, his sister's fiancé, said, as he followed her from the kitchen and deposited a dish full of crispy brown roast potatoes in the middle of the dining table.

It all looks so delicious. "Thanks, guys," Fitzwilliam said as he reached for a plate piled high with balls made of pork meat, sage, and onion.

"Don't thank me, Rich." Elise pulled out a chair opposite him and sat down. "I merely chopped the veg and warmed the plates. Rhys did all the hard work." She looked round at the dark-haired brick house of a man sitting down by her side and blew him a kiss.

"If I'd left it to you, we'd be having fish finger sandwiches for dinner." His gentle chuckle and softly lilting Welsh accent took any sting out of the comment.

Elise laughed. "And what's wrong with fish finger sandwiches? They were Rich's favourite when he was younger."

"Can't beat them." Fitzwilliam nodded as he reached for the dish containing bright orange carrots glistening with melted butter and sprinkled with chopped parsley.

"There's nothing wrong with fish finger sandwiches, *cariad*, but I don't think they're traditional enough for Christmas Day." Rhys grabbed her hand and kissed the tips of her fingers before dropping them and grabbing the gravy boat. "And besides," he continued, pouring gravy over his turkey, "your poor brother here has been working hard all day keeping us safe from that bunch of lunatics in the royal family. He needs something more substantial." He grinned at Fitzwilliam, then quickly dodged out of the way of Elise's hand as it swiped at his head.

"How many times do I have to tell you, it's his job to protect them from us, not us from them!" She giggled as she reached behind her to the sideboard and picked up one of the three bottles of red wine Fitzwilliam had brought with him. She poured herself and Rhys a generous glass each, then offered the bottle to her brother. "Are you able to have a glass of wine?"

"Just a small one, please. I'm still on call until midnight, so I need to stay sober in case I have to drive anywhere." He accepted the gravy from Rhys and poured the thick brown sauce over his vegetables. He looked at his plate. *Yummy!* A huge grin spread over his face. He picked up his wineglass and raised it for a toast. "Happy Christmas to my favourite sister—"

"Your *only* sister." Elise stuck her tongue out at him.

"—and her talented better half. Thank you for inviting me."

They raised their glasses in his direction and drank.

"I spoke to Mum just now," Fitzwilliam told Elise as he lifted his fork to his mouth.

"I hope Desperate Dougie and his freeloading family have dragged themselves away from the pub. When I rang her just before three, they still hadn't turned up." She huffed and shoved a whole roast potato into her mouth.

"Yes, they arrived halfway through the King's Speech, I believe." He shook his head and stabbed a Brussels sprout with his fork.

"Cheeky," Rhys murmured through a mouthful of food.

"It's ridiculous," she scoffed. "They take her for granted while she cooks and cleans for them and then provides them with somewhere to pass out drunk. I really hoped this year she would come and stay with us, but it appears she would rather run around after a useless man and his family than visit her two children." She put down her fork and bowed her head.

Rhys leaned over and patted Elise's arm. "*Caraid*, don't do this to yourself. You know that's not how she thinks. She wants to be where she's needed, and Dougie needs her."

She scraped her hand over her cheek. "To cook for him, clean for him, and look after his stupid relations!" she cried, then shook her head. "Why can't she see he's using her?"

"She just can't," Fitzwilliam said. "And lord knows we've tried. She can't help herself. She can't cope without a man to look after, however undeserving he may be." He cut into his last slice of succulent turkey and smiled at his younger sibling. "I think she's happy in a strange sort of way." His mother seemed to accept her life of servitude; her only ambition was to make the man she loved happy. *Maybe that's where I'm going wrong with Amber?* Should I care more about making her happy than I do about my job? *Why do I have to choose?* He sighed. *I want to do both!*

"Well, at least this one doesn't beat her," Rhys said, breaking the silence.

"Good point." Fitzwilliam nodded. Their mother's last ex had been a brute of a man. Not just lazy but aggressive too. Dougie, as desperate as he was for an easy life, didn't seem to be the violent type. He was more likely to fall asleep in front of the television in a beer coma than lift his hand to her in a drunken rage. *She's probably much better off with this one.*

"Yes, I suppose you're right." Elise looked at Rich and shrugged. "Desperate Dougie could be worse."

Fitzwilliam undid the top button on his jeans and made himself comfy in a brown leather armchair in the open plan seating area of his sister's flat. He let out an enormous sigh. "God, I'm stuffed," he informed his future brother-in-law, who was lounging on a large cream sofa opposite him.

Rhys, his beefy frame too large for the two-seater (his feet had to rest on the arm), nodded and sighed in return.

Elise walked over with a mug of black coffee and placed it on the small side table next to her brother. He smiled up at her. "Thanks, sis."

She picked up her fiancé's head as she sat down on the sofa, releasing it to rest on her lap.

"Have you two set a wedding date yet?" Picking up the steaming cup of coffee, Fitzwilliam blew on the top of the dark liquid.

"Actually, we have a date in mind — Saturday, the eighth of July. Rhys has no club or national games scheduled two weeks on either side of that date, so we have everything pencilled in. We need to do a final check with Rhys's agent when he gets back after the break, and then we can get organised."

Fitzwilliam nodded. His future brother-in-law was one of the brightest up and coming professional Welsh rugby players at the moment, and he was much in demand. "That sounds good. I'll book leave when I'm in the office on Tuesday."

"You will give me away, won't you, Rich?" Her

blue eyes stared at him, searching his face. Then she shrugged. "Even if Dad turns up, I don't want him taking credit for me. It's down to you, not him, that I've turned out reasonably sane and generally law-abiding."

"Except when you drive, *cariad*!" her fiancé butted in.

"That's why I said *generally.*" She giggled.

Fitzwilliam smiled at his sister. He understood her need not to give their father any recognition for raising his children. Even before he'd disappeared, he'd been an absent father at best. Happy to throw money at his wife to keep her and their young children amused, he'd rarely taken the time away from his business to actually spend time with them. *It's a wonder Elise has turned out as well as she has.* Leaving them when she was only three years old, Eric Fitzwilliam had disappeared for five years before resurfacing and begging his wife for forgiveness. In a rare display of confidence, his mother had refused to take him back but had allowed him to see the children once a month. Although Fitzwilliam had been excited to spend time with his father, Elise had been more wary and less forgiving, frequently refusing to see him. *Rightly so, as it turned out.* Ten years ago, he'd disappeared again. No one had heard from him since.

"Will you, Rich?" Elise's slightly unsteady voice dragged him back to the present.

"Sorry, sis. Of course I will if that's what you want," he replied.

She nodded. "I'm going to ask Amber to be my matron of honour. Have you spoken to her today?" She tilted her head to one side, her eyebrows raised.

"Yes. We spoke briefly this morning. She was a bit hungover. She was out with old school friends last night." He smiled. *Thank goodness she's having fun without me.* He'd been relieved to hear his wife was having a good time staying with her parents. He felt less guilty for not being there. "Anyway" — he glanced at his watch— "it's almost eleven. Only another hour, and I'm a free man for twenty-four hours. I'll be with her soon."

"Are you driving to Kent early in the morning?" Rhys asked.

Fitzwilliam nodded. "I hope to get there in time for breakfast so I can have the whole day there. The plan is for us to ditch her family at some stage and maybe go for a walk along the beach together." *It will be nice to have some time for ourselves.* He missed his wife.

Elise smiled at him and then turned to her boyfriend. "I'd love a hot chocolate, darling. The one Rich bought me for Christmas, please. Oh, and maybe one of those brownies you made yesterday?" Fitzwilliam thought he saw her wink at Rhys as he rose.

"Sounds good. Do you want anything, Rich?"

Fitzwilliam shook his head. "No thanks, mate. I'll need to get going soon."

Watching her fiancé leave the room, Elise turned to her brother. "Is everything okay with you and Amber, Rich?"

Where did that come from? He frowned. "Yes, we're fine. Why do you ask?"

"She popped over the evening before she left. I think you were working. Rhys was in Cardiff, so it was just the two of us. She was *really* upset you were having to work over Christmas and New Year again this year. Like spitting feathers upset. She complained other people had asked for time off and got it. She said you didn't seem bothered."

Hell's teeth! She just won't let it go. And now she'd gone bleating to his sister about it. *It's not my fault!* He crossed his arms. "That's not true. I do care. But I'm still a newbie in my section, so everyone else gets priority over me. I asked for leave, but someone got there before me."

"Well, whatever actually happened, she was pretty hacked off, Rich."

Don't I know it! He sighed. "Yes, I know. She was still pretty mad at me when she left."

"So what are you going to do to fix it?" Elise asked, her eyes wide with concern.

"Fix what? I can't get the time off right now, sis. It's that simple." He glared at her. Why was she interfering? *I don't need another woman telling me I'm a bad husband!*

"Okay, Rich. I get it. I'm sorry." She put her hands out in front of her, palms facing him. "I'm not trying to butt in. I just wanted to make sure you were aware of how she feels. It's not just that you can't get the time off. She thinks you don't care about spending time with her. She's worried all you care about is your job and getting a promotion."

But I'm doing this for us! "It's not *all* I care about, sis. But it's important I keep my head down at this stage in my career and learn as much as I can. I've never been one to sit on my laurels and wait for promotion. You know that. I like to make it happen. The way to do that is to put the hours in. Amber knows that. She had the same attitude when we first met." He uncrossed his arms and scratched his spiky chin. "But lately, she's lost interest in her career, and suddenly, it's a bad thing to be ambitious. I can't win!"

"I understand your frustration, and I don't have

an answer. But I'm just warning you because men sometimes don't realise there's a problem until it's too late. I don't want that to happen to you and Amber," she said, her voice breaking.

Fitzwilliam's gaze softened, and he smiled at her. "Please don't worry, El. I do care that she's unhappy, and I know she wants us to spend more quality time together. I'm hoping if everyone comes back from leave as planned and nothing big kicks off, then I'll be able to take time off for the last week she's on leave. We'll go somewhere, just the two of us, for a few days."

She sniffed, then frowned at him, her head on one side. "You keep talking about what *she* wants. What about you, Rich? What do *you* want?"

"I want to get back into my wife's good books, sis. I want the arguing to stop and for us to go back to how we were."

LATE EVENING, SATURDAY 31 DECEMBER

"Is that all, your lordship?" Fraser walked back across the drawing room of The Dower House to the trolley and stood facing James, waiting to be dismissed.

"Yes, thank you, Fraser. That will be all tonight. And a happy New Year to you and Mrs Fraser."

Fraser bowed. "Thank you, my lord. I wish you and Lady Rossex the best for the coming new year."

Bea smiled at the butler as he straightened up. "And enjoy your day off tomorrow."

"Thank you, my lady. Goodnight." The butler glided from the room and closed the door behind him.

"Are the Frasers off tomorrow?" James asked.

"Yes. We're at Fenn House all day, and Sarah has invited us over for supper tomorrow evening. It made sense to let them have a day off. Mrs Fraser told me this morning they're going to visit her nephew and family in Lincolnshire." She walked across the drawing room and sat on the sofa opposite her husband and Penny, their Labrador.

She sighed as she relaxed back into the chair. *Why do I feel so drained*? If she was honest, she just wanted to go to bed. Her husband poured her a black coffee and stretched over the coffee table to pass it to her.

"Are you all right, sweetheart?" His brow cracked, his eyebrows elevating as he searched her face. *He looks concerned. That's nice.*

She smiled. "Yes, just tired." Leaning forward, she took the cup from him.

"You look pale, and I noticed you ate little at dinner."

He noticed then? She was pleased. Something had distracted him when they had been at Francis Court earlier in the evening for the traditional family New Year's Eve get together. Distracted like he'd been for weeks. She worried about Sarah's comment last week when she'd asked if James could be having an affair. Was their marriage in trouble, and she'd not even realised? She dismissed the thought as quickly as it had popped into her head. *He's not too distracted to still care about me. He's probably just tired, like I am.*

She hoped she would get her appetite back soon. Her mother had commented on how thin she looked only this morning. If she got too thin, the papers would no doubt speculate she was overdoing a diet or working out too much. *They always have an opinion!*

"I didn't fancy it. I think I ate too much at lunch. It's all been such a rush today. After we arrived home and changed from our walk with your parents, it felt like it was only five minutes before we were getting ready to go out for dinner."

He nodded.

She continued, "I love spending time with our families, but it's been full on since the earl and countess arrived." She sipped her coffee and shook her head when he offered her a biscuit.

"I know what you mean," he agreed. "It's been great having my parents here, but I must confess I'm looking forward to Monday when they leave and we have this place to ourselves again."

Penny sat up as James got up and strolled over to the drinks cabinet, where he poured himself a whisky. "Do you want one, sweetheart?" he called over his shoulder.

Her stomach turned at the thought of alcohol. She hadn't even finished her wine at dinner. She usually enjoyed a decent glass of red, preferring it over spirits, but she didn't want anything today. "No thanks, darling."

Should I see the doctor if this loss of appetite doesn't go soon? She didn't want to make a fuss or worry James. She was sure it was just all the overeating they'd done over the last week.

"Sweetheart, did you hear me?" James had returned to his seat opposite her and was now staring, his hand resting on still-sitting Penny's head, waiting for a response.

"Sorry, darling, what did you say?"

"I said we're about to go into a new year. Are you making any resolutions this year?" James raised his glass to his lips and took a sip of the amber liquid.

She frowned. "I'm not sure there's any point. They never survive more than a few days before they're broken. Look at what happened last year, for example. I said I was going to learn to say no to my mother more often. I resolved to stop letting her persuade me to take on her causes and instead let me find some of my own." She huffed. "And by

January the fifth, I'd agreed to be on a committee to save that ugly folly on the outskirts of Fawstead. I don't know how she does it." She raked her hands through her long auburn hair, and her husband laughed.

"She's a witch!" he cried, raising his drink in the air. "You know, that's the only explanation that makes sense. Look how she manipulated me into agreeing to attend the charity committee meeting in London next week on her behalf." He pinched his mouth and raised his voice. "James, you're so good with the old ladies on the board. If anyone can per-suade them a fairy-themed gala dinner will be a dis-aster, you can, darling."

Penny stood up and gave a low *woof*, her tail wagging as Bea laughed out loud at his impression of her mother. He had her off to a tee. "It sounds like we both need to give it another go this year." She raised her coffee cup to him. "Here's to a joint New Year's resolution to say no to my mother!"

James raised his whisky glass high. "Hear, hear." He patted Penny's grey-speckled black head, and she settled down at his feet.

They smiled at each other across the coffee ta-ble. *He really has the most amazing smile. I'm so lucky.* She continued looking into her husband's grey eyes, then he broke their connection and looked away. Crossing his legs and leaning back into the armchair, he gazed at his glass. *Something is still bothering him. I wish he'd tell me what's up and not just tell me he's fine.* If he didn't tell her soon, she would have to have it out with him. But not tonight; tonight she was exhausted.

Rising from the sofa, she put her coffee cup on the table. "Darling, do you mind if I go up now?"

"No, you go. I'm going to finish my drink and read a bit. I'll be up later."

James watched his wife as she left the room. She was getting thin these days, and he was worried about her. He sighed. *I will have to talk to her about seeing a doctor in the new year.*

He stared down at the now empty glass in his hand. He rose and walked over to the drinks cabinet to refill it. *Last one, then I'll call it a day.* Once they got tomorrow over and said goodbye to his parents, he would have to concentrate on the week ahead. He had decisions to make. He was worried about how the next week would pan out. Especially if his wife was ill.

As he returned to his seat, he patted Penny on the head and said quietly, "I don't suppose it will help when I tell her what's really on my mind, will it, old girl?"

Penny looked up at her master with adoring eyes. She would forgive him anything. *But will Bea?*

9

MEANWHILE, SATURDAY 31 DECEMBER

"I really wish you were here."

Fitzwilliam moved the phone further away from his ear as his wife shouted into her mobile at the other end of the line. "I do too," he replied, unsure if she could hear him over the background noise. "Where did you say you are again?"

There was a pause, and she shouted, "Another gin and tonic, please," to someone in the background.

"Sorry, what did you say?" she hollered back.

He sighed. "Where. Are. You?" he raised his voice and enunciated each word as best he could.

"We're at a pub in town. It's so packed, the bouncers have stopped letting any more people in. Let me find out if it's quieter in the loos."

She repeatedly said, "Excuse me," as he imagined her making her way through the throng of partygoers to get to the toilets.

"Is that better?"

"Yes, I can hear you now."

"I can't wait for you to be here, Rich. I've found this amazing cottage along the coast. There's a view of the sea from the bedroom window, and it's less than a five-minute walk to the beach." She blurted it out so quickly she was almost breathless.

What a relief to hear her sounding so excited. He'd been busy at work since he'd returned from seeing her on Boxing Day. That, combined with Amber having been out frequently catching up with old friends, meant they'd barely spoken since. Although their day together had been pleasant, they'd spent it with her family, and they'd not had much time to talk alone. His plan of going for a walk together and clearing the air hadn't materialised. He was worried she was still harbouring some resentment against him. But now it sounded as if all was well.

"It sounds great. I'm really looking forward to it," he told her.

"So when do you think you'll get here? I've booked the cottage for four days from Friday."

"I should be able to finish on Thursday. I can

come up to your parents on Thursday night, and we can go to the cottage on Friday morning."

"That's perfect. Oh, Rich, it will be so good to have time together. I've missed you." A door slammed at her end, and a woman's voice screamed, "Amber, are you coming? The DJ's about to start."

He smiled. "I've missed you too, bird. Now go and enjoy the rest of your evening. I'll speak to you in the morning."

"Okay, I hope you don't get called out. I love you."

"I love you too," he shouted, although the music now pumping out in the background made it hard to know if she actually heard him.

10

MID-AFTERNOON, SUNDAY 1 JANUARY

The Society Page online article:

<u>Countess of Rossex Absent from Fenn House Lunch</u>

Today, King Henry and Queen Mary hosted their traditional New Year's Day lunch at their Fenshire home Fenn House. Joining the king and queen were their children and their families. The Earl and Countess of Durrland, great friends of the Prince of Wales and his wife, were also present, accompanying their son James Wiltshire (24), the Earl of Rossex.

In the morning, all members of the party attended the Sunday service at St Stephen's Church, with the younger generation walking there and back, greeting the crowds along the route. One notable absentee was Lady Beatrice (21), the Countess of Rossex. A statement released at lunchtime from Gollingham Palace reported Lady Beatrice is currently ill with a suspected sickness bug and will not be attending any public commitments for the next three days while she rests at home. Everyone here at TSP wishes her a speedy recovery.

"So how was New Year's Eve?" James looked down at the woman walking beside him.

Gill Sterling lifted her head towards him, her long brown hair flying around her face as she swiped it away with her hand. "It was quiet. Alex went to The Ship and Seal in the village, but I didn't fancy it, so I stayed in and watched a film." She pulled the fur collar of her anorak up around her neck and smiled. "What about you?"

"We had dinner up at the main house"—he nodded towards Francis Court, visible between the trees—"with Bea's parents, her siblings, and my parents." He stopped, then looking around, he raised his fingers to his lips and whistled. "Penny," he shouted into the undergrowth. The crackle of leaves and broken twigs heralded the arrival of the black Labrador, who ran to her master and sat in front of him, her tail wagging.

He patted her head. "Good girl." Reaching into the pocket of his Barbour jacket, he pulled out a treat and gave it to her. He smiled at his companion. "Sorry, I don't want her going far today." He glanced at his watch. "It's three-thirty already, and it'll be dark soon."

She nodded, and they carried on walking.

"I read online Lady Beatrice didn't make it to lunch with the king and queen today. I hope she's feeling better?"

"She appears to have picked up a sickness bug. She's been out of sorts for a few days now. Of course, she's been pushing through it, like she does, but this morning, she really wasn't looking well. I insisted she stay at home and rest." He sighed. He would have to push for her to called the doctor soon if she didn't recover in the next few days even if she continued to tell him she was fine. *She's so determined!* "I know she must be poorly as she didn't argue at all." He chuckled. "She's feeling better this afternoon, and hopefully, she'll eat something tonight."

"Is it your parents' last night here?" Gill looked

over, her blue eyes watering as she moved her face away from the wind.

"Yes, they leave tomorrow afternoon."

"Then do you have a busy few days ahead, or is it a quiet start to the year for you?"

He looked down at the black Labrador by his side. Bending down, he clipped her lead onto her harness. "Good girl, Penny." Darkness was falling, and he couldn't be sure what was in the shadows. *That will at least stop her darting off after any deer.* "I think we should make our way back now," he said as he tucked his scarf into the top of his coat with one hand.

"James, did you hear me?"

"Sorry, I was thinking about how late it's getting. What did you say?"

"I asked if you have a slow start to the new year?"

"Well, normally, yes. But when I mentioned at dinner the other night I was going to be in London on Wednesday for a meeting, my extremely persuasive mother-in-law roped me in to going up a day early and attending a charity meeting on her behalf. She says she needs me to schmooze the committee into abandoning a theme she thinks is unsuitable for an event she's sponsoring in the summer." He huffed and shook his head, then looked over at

Penny, her nose deep in a pile of leaves, and gently tugged her to him as they continued on.

"I'm curious. Do you have security with you when you attend these functions and meetings?"

"It all depends on if what I'm doing is private or public duties."

Gill frowned up at him.

"So, for example, the engagement I have on Wednesday morning is private, so if I was going up only for that, then I would drive myself there and back, no fuss. However, the charity committee meeting I'm attending on Tuesday afternoon is classed as public duties as I'm representing Princess Helen. So for that, I'll have royal protection with me. And to complicate it further, although I'm still driving myself to London on Tuesday, I'm giving Bea's brother Fred a lift, so we'll have a police escort."

"It sounds very complicated."

"You get used to it." He shrugged. "It comes with the job." They came out of the woods and headed towards the staff cottages. Gill slowed down, then stopped.

"Are you all right?" he asked. She seemed reluctant to move. He'd noticed earlier she was being quieter than usual. *I hope things aren't getting worse for her at home.*

"Yes." She sighed and touched his arm. "It's just that I've really enjoyed this walk so much, and I'm not keen to go back." She removed her hand from his coat and hugged her arms around herself, staring at the ground.

She looks so defeated. He wondered what to say to make her feel better. He reached out and put a hand on her shoulder. "It won't be long now." *I hope that reassures her.*

She nodded, and head still down, she thrust her hands into the pockets of her coat. "I know," she responded softly. "Alex is getting worse. He watches my every move."

She looked up into James's face. He could see the faint smudge of an old bruise on her cheek. He winced.

"I wasn't even sure I could get away this afternoon," she said. "But fortunately he had to inspect some damage that had happened to one of the cottages last night." She took one hand out of her pocket and looked at her watch. "I need to go. He'll be on his way back soon. I don't want to risk him seeing us together. If he did, I dread to think what he might do."

11

LATE AFTERNOON, TUESDAY 3 JANUARY

"Pregnant?" Bea, the Countess of Rossex, cried, spitting out her tea.

Penny, startled by the spray of tea engulfing her, leapt up from where she'd been laying by Bea's feet in the morning room at The Dower House and moved away, turning her head this way and that, as if trying to work out what had happened. Bea whispered, "Sorry." Leaning over to Penny, now stood by her feet, looking up into her eyes, she patted her grey-speckled black head. The Labrador closed her eyes, then turned and lay down again.

"Shush," Sarah scolded her, looking over at the sleeping baby in the bassinet by her side on the other sofa opposite her sister. "You'll wake Robbie."

Bea turned to her sister, ready to say, "Well, what do you expect when you throw a word like that out at me?" but thought better of it and instead said, "Sorry."

"Surely it must have crossed your mind, Bea? It's obvious to me you have morning sickness," Sarah whispered as she grabbed a napkin from the tea tray laid out on the coffee table between them and handed it to her sister.

Bea received it with a shaky hand and wiped down the front of her black T-shirt. She shook her head. "It honestly never occurred to me. I assumed it was a bug."

Sarah held out a fist and raised her fingers one by one as she said, "First, you've lost your appetite. Next, you feel sick, especially first thing in the morning, and third, you're exhausted all the time." She put her hand down on her lap. "It's been a couple of weeks now, Bea, not just a few days. There's no doubt in my mind." She leaned over her sleeping three-month-old son and retrieved a blue-and-white rectangular box that had been tucked behind the blanket covering him.

"There's only one way to find out," she said as she handed it to Bea.

Bea looked down at the box before her. *Oh my goodness!* A wave of nausea washed over her. She raised her other hand to her mouth. "A pregnancy test?"

"Yes." Her sister nodded. "And make sure you do it right first time. It wasn't easy to get hold of one, I can tell you. I had to ask Ma's maid, Naomi, to get it this morning from the large supermarket in King's Town. Let's hope no one recognised her."

She raised her eyebrows, and Bea nodded in return. Her sister was right. *The last thing I need right now is for the press to find out and start speculating.* She turned the box over in her hand and tried to read the instructions on the back, but her eyes wouldn't focus. *I can't be pregnant, can I?* Although she and James had been married for a year, neither of them wanted to rush into starting a family. They were both still young and were keen to travel and explore the world.

"But I'm on the pill, Sarah," she told her sister as she opened the box and removed the fat white pen-like object from inside.

"Well, it's never one-hundred-percent safe. And anyway, didn't you have that horrid tummy bug that was going around shortly after Robbie was born?"

"Yes, but it only lasted a few days." She returned the object back to the box.

"I know, but sometimes that's all it takes. Now go to the bathroom and take the test."

"But—"

"No buts, Bea. It's simple. You wee on the stick, and if you get a blue line, then you're pregnant." She waved her hand towards the open door. "Go on!"

Bea dragged herself up from the sofa and, box in hand, headed for the downstairs cloakroom.

"Well?" Sarah jumped up as her sister walked back into the morning room fifteen minutes later.

Bea slowly lowered herself onto the sofa opposite her sister. She patted Penny on the head, and reaching over, she touched the coffee pot. It was lukewarm. It would have to do. She lifted it up and poured herself a coffee. *Breathe, Bea. Just breathe.*

"Bea!" Sarah hissed, sitting back down and quickly glancing over at Robbie, his tiny hands curled into fists and his legs twitching as he slept.

Bea lowered the coffee cup from her lips and allowed a smile to spread slowly across her face. Her sister jumped up and rushed around the table to envelop her in an enormous hug.

"I'm so pleased, Bea. It's going to be marvellous to raise our children together."

Bea struggled out of her sister's hold and

grabbed her arms, looking deep into her watery brown eyes. *Why can't I stop smiling?* But then her smile faded as reality hit. *How am I going to cope with this?* "Promise me you'll help, Sarah. I've no idea what to do. This wasn't part of our plans right now." Her face flushed. "I'm scared." She put her head in her hands and shook her head. "And I don't want to be the size of an elephant," she whinged as she looked up again.

Sarah wiped her hand under her eyes and laughed. "Of course I'll help you, silly." She held her little sister at arm's length and grinned. "And I know you're going to be one of those annoying women who are so slim, you only know they're pregnant when you see them from the side. Unlike me, who, if you remember, looked like I was slowly being blown up by a foot pump for six months." They both laughed and hugged each other.

"So when will you tell James?" Sarah rose and moved over to check on Robbie.

Oh my goodness—James! How would he feel about this? She knew he would be supportive, but would he *really* want this child? Or would he just accept it as he did everything that was asked of him?

Bea shook her head. "I haven't even thought about it yet. I'm totally unprepared for this moment." She leaned back on the sofa. *He's going to be even more shocked than me.* "How on earth do I break the news to him?" she asked in a shaky voice that was barely audible. Penny, alerted by Bea's distress, jumped up on the sofa and tried to lick her face.

"Penny, get off the sofa," Sarah commanded.

Bea gave Penny a quick kiss on the side of her head and pushed her gently down. *Well, I can't tell him on the phone, that's for sure.* That would be unfair to him. "I think I'd prefer to tell him in person. It'll be an enormous shock for him too."

"When's he back?"

"Tomorrow. He has that charity committee thing he's doing for Ma later this afternoon, then a couple of meetings in the morning. He said he would come straight back after that." She fiddled with her wedding ring. "What will I say to him when I talk to him tonight on the phone? He's bound to ask me how I am."

"Just tell him you're feeling better and looking forward to getting back to work next week. Then he won't worry, and you can surprise him with the good news when he's back. I'm sure he'll be really excited, sis."

"All right, but I don't want anyone else to know until after I've told him. You need to promise to keep quiet until then," she pleaded with her sister. "You can't even tell John. And you *definitely* can't tell Ma. Promise?"

"Promise," Sarah agreed.

"Look out for the car!" the woman cried.

What the? James instinctively tugged the steering wheel sharply to the right to avoid the object blocking the road.

He was aware of the screeching of tyres on tarmac as he fought to keep control of the car, but it was no good. The Audi had a mind of its own as it bounced along the rough grass by the side of the road.

If I can just keep it from...

But there was nothing he could do. The car plunged down the shallow embankment, rolling over once, twice. *Boom!* It eventually stopped when it ploughed into a two-hundred-year-old oak tree.

12

12:30 AM, WEDNESDAY 4 JANUARY

"Slow down, Terry!" Kim Maynard cried as a large deer, running across the narrow Fenshire country road ten metres ahead of them, was illuminated in the car headlights. Her husband hit the brakes on his five series BMW, and as they slowed down, the animal dived into the hedge on their right and disappeared into the trees behind it.

"That was close." Her husband let out a rush of air. He returned his foot to the accelerator pedal but kept his speed below thirty as they rounded the next corner.

"You never know when one is going to bolt across your path around here. You know that," she admonished him.

He nodded. "Sorry, dear. It's been such a long

time since we've been out this late at night. I forgot how many of them move around when it gets dark."

"You're right," she agreed. "I wouldn't normally want to have dinner with the Hamilton's on a school night. You know what they're like since he retired. They forget the rest of us need to get up for work. But I felt bad when we had to cancel on them at the last minute when you had that tummy bug. I thought it would be rude to say no."

"I'm glad you didn't. It was a good night and —" He stopped talking and slowed down, peering into the darkness ahead. "What's that over there?" He removed one hand from the steering wheel and pointed about twenty metres ahead on the right where the faint headlights of a car illuminated the trunk of a large oak tree.

"Call the emergency services," Terry Maynard barked at his wife as he jumped out of the car.

Watching him dash across the road, the headlights of the BMW lighting his diagonal path towards the tree, Kim reached back into the footwell behind the driver's seat and yanked her handbag towards herself. *Oh my life, what's happened?* With shaking hands, she unzipped the inside pocket and retrieved her mobile phone. *Breathe!* She flipped open her phone and pressed the buttons. Nine. Nine. Nine. A wave of nausea washed over her. She searched around the car and spotted a bottle of water in the side pocket by her husband's car seat. She leaned over and, unscrewing the top, took a huge gulp of water. *Ah, I needed that.* As her still unsteady hands tried to put the lid back on, she dropped it. *Drat!* She searched for it in the dark.

"Emergency Services. What is your emergency?"

The voice brought her back to the phone, the bottle top forgotten.

She took a deep breath. "There's been a dreadful accident."

Kim walked across the road on wobbly legs, her mobile phone glued to her ear.

The voice on the other end of the line was soothing and calm. "The police and an ambulance are on their way. What's happening now, Mrs Maynard?"

She didn't really want to look. *What happens if there are body parts scattered around?* She felt sick. *Pull yourself together. Someone needs your help.* She peered down the embankment. "My husband is leaning into the passenger side of the car." She gulped. "The car's a real mess. It looks like it went straight into the tree." Her husband's voice sounded as she scrambled down the grassy side. "I think my husband is talking to someone," she told the emergency operator as she stopped and looked towards the scene of the accident.

Terry's head peered around the door. "Did you get an ambulance?" he shouted as he moved towards her and clambered up the ditch.

"Yes, darling. They should be here any minute."

As he approached her, the light of the car's headlights picked out his pale face. Two spots of red brightened his cheeks. *He looks worried.* He held out his hand, and she passed the phone to him.

"This is Terry Maynard," he told the operator. "I have checked inside the car. The driver is done for. I couldn't get to him. The door won't open. His side took the brunt of the impact. I leaned over from the passenger side to reach him, but there's no pulse. I've turned the ignition off. The passenger, a woman, is still just alive. She's unconscious, but she has a very faint pulse. I can't move her safely. It's a bit of a mess inside the car. She's well and truly trapped. You'll need to alert the fire service."

"Yes, sir. They are on their way too."

"Well, I hope they're quick. I'm not sure she's going to make it."

———

Kim pulled the blanket tighter around herself, willing her body to stop shivering. The wool blanket was scratchy against her face. She blew it away from her skin. Looking towards the tree, she put her hand up to her temple to block out the bright lights now surrounding it. *I hope she's still alive in there.* The noise from the cutting machinery dominated the night, occasionally broken by shouts from the firefighters working on the car.

Two men walked towards her. She recognised her husband on the left. The other one looked like the man she'd spoken to earlier when the police had first arrived on scene.

She rose from the open boot of the police estate car, where she'd been sitting, and got unsteadily to her feet. Her husband gave her a weary smile. *Oh, Terry, this has been awful for you.* He held out his arms as he reached her, and she launched herself into them, desperate for the familiarity and comfort they would bring.

"Are you okay, Mrs Maynard?" The police sergeant took off his hat and let his arm drop by his side.

Kim raised her head from her husband's shoulder and nodded. Terry released his grip on her as the man addressed them.

"Thank you for your help, Mr and Mrs Maynard. We have your brief statement, Mr Maynard, but we will need a more detailed one from both of you tomorrow, if that's all right?" They nodded in unison. "Someone from Fenshire CID will be in touch in the morning to arrange it with you. In the meantime, we won't keep you any longer."

"Is she still alive?" Kim blurted out.

The policeman nodded. "The helicopter will fly her to the hospital in King's Town as soon as they've cut her out," he informed them.

"And him?"

He shook his head. "I'm afraid not. There's nothing that can be done for him, but they will cut him out anyway to retrieve the body."

He sounded matter of fact. *I suppose he has to deal with incidents like this a lot.* Maybe they become detached to help them deal with it all. She shuddered, and her husband's arms tightened around her.

The policeman returned his hat to his head. "Are you sure you're okay to drive, Mr Maynard?"

"Yes, it's not far."

"I'll get one of the cars here to escort you home." He stopped. A young policeman shouted as he ran in their direction.

"Sorry to interrupt, sir, but we have an issue," he said as he drew near, slightly out of breath. "Can you come now, please, sarge?"

"Okay, Matthews. I'll be right over." He turned back to them. "Sorry about that, but it looks like I need to go. As I was saying, I'll get one of the patrol cars to follow you home. Again, thank you and good evening."

He strode off towards the lights and stopped at a police car on the way, pointing towards them.

"Come on, Kim, let's get you home," Terry said to his wife as he opened the passenger door for her.

Yes, please. I need to be away from here. As she got in, she worried about why the sergeant had been called away so suddenly. *Oh no!* "Do you think she died?"

Her husband started the engine. He shook his head and turned to look at her. "No, I think they've just confirmed the driver's identity."

Her eyes wide open, Kim whispered to him, "Who?"

"I'm fairly sure it was the Earl of Rossex."

13

3:30 AM, WEDNESDAY 4 JANUARY

Detective Sergeant Richard Fitzwilliam of the Protection and Investigation (Royal) Service walked down the corridor of the security building at Gollingham Palace. He'd done his fair share of late nights recently, and normally it was deserted at this time of the morning. The offices locked and empty. The only lights coming from the open plan area at the end, where those who were on duty kept themselves busy until they were relieved. But tonight it was different. Lights were on. Offices were open. Whispered conversations were barely audible as he passed. He turned into the last office on the right and stood in front of the desk.

Detective Chief Inspector Frances Copson was

on the phone. She nodded to Fitzwilliam and indicated for him to take a seat.

"Yes, sir. He's just arrived, and I'm going to talk to him now. I'll get back to you as soon as I can." She leaned back in her chair and tucked her long black hair behind her ear with her left hand. "Yes, sir, I appreciate the urgency." She rolled her eyes at Fitzwilliam. "I'll get back to you ASAP." She sat upright and pulled her chair forward, towards her desk. "Yes, sir. Thank you." She held on to the handset and huffed before pressing a button on the mini switchboard in front of her. "Janet, please hold any calls until I tell you otherwise and let Mr Goody know I will ring him back in fifteen minutes. Thank you." She pressed another button and returned the handset to its cradle.

"Goody? As in principle private secretary to the king?"

"Yes, Fitzwilliam. We have what they refer to in films as 'a situation'." She used her fingers to air quote the phrase, then pushed her tortoise-shell glasses further up the bridge of her nose. "The Earl of Rossex has been killed in a car accident near Francis Court."

Fitzwilliam's eyes shot open wide. *Hells bells! That's more than a situation. That's a major incident!*

"That's about as much as I have at the moment," his boss continued. "The emergency services are finishing up on-site now. They had to cut him out of the car." She shook her head. "Not that it helped at all. He was already dead before they got to him." She shifted in her seat. "We have a voluntary media blackout agreed at the moment, but how long it will last is anyone's guess. If the international press gets hold of the story, then all bets will be off. We're lucky it's the early hours of the morning. That should help to keep a lid on it for a little while yet."

He nodded. The longer they could keep the press in the dark, the better.

She rose from her desk and pushed her arms out in front of her. Fitzwilliam made to get up, but she waved him back down. "Sorry, I just need to stretch. I've been trapped at my desk since I received the call a couple of hours ago. This is only my second royal family death since I've been in PaIRS, and I forgot what an intense experience it is." She sat again, moving her head from side to side. *Crack* "Ah, that's better."

"So do we think it's a terrorist attack, ma'am?"

Copson jolted upright, then shook her head, frowning. "No. As far as we know, it's a straightforward accident. Why do you ask, Fitzwilliam?"

Now *he* was frowning. *Why did she call me then?* "Sorry, ma'am. I just assumed it must be if you called me in given I work in Intelligence."

"Ah, I see." She nodded her head. "Yes, of course. I can see why you would think that."

Well, that hasn't helped me at all. He waited patiently for her to explain.

"So here's the thing, Fitzwilliam. Detective Chief Inspector Angus Reed — do you know him, by the way?"

Fitzwilliam shook his head. *Where is this going?*

She continued, "He heads up the team who is going to be overseeing the investigation into the earl's death. But he's one man down. One of his guys is on leave, and they can't get hold of him because he's on the top of a mountain somewhere." She shook her head. "The Super asked me if I have anyone in my team I can recommend to be temporarily transferred over to bring Reed up to full complement." Copson stopped and looked expectantly at Fitzwilliam.

"Me?" *Surely not me? I've not done any investigation within PaIRS. I'll be next to useless.*

"Yes, you, Fitzwilliam. I think it will be good experience for you. It's a high-profile investigation with direct contact with the royals, neither of which you have experience of yet—"

"But it's an investigation, ma'am," Fitzwilliam interrupted. "And my only experience is in intelligence."

"Yes, I'm aware of that. But if you really want to progress in this organisation, you need to widen your skill set. This is a splendid chance for you to do that."

Her steely look was slightly unnerving.

Fitzwilliam looked away, his mind in a quandary. *I get it's a fantastic opportunity. But am I ready for it?* "Won't my lack of experience be a problem for DCI Reed?"

"Reed doesn't need to read your resume, Fitzwilliam. This is being done on my recommendation, and that's good enough for him. So what do you—" The phone in front of her rang, and she sighed, picking it up. "Yes, Janet? I thought I asked you to hold all calls?" Her frown disappeared, and her face softened. "Okay, just a second." She held her hand over the mouthpiece, then looking up at Fitzwilliam, said, "I must take this call, Fitzwilliam. You have fifteen minutes to give this offer some thought and give me your answer. Off you go."

Fitzwilliam nodded. "Ma'am," he said as he turned and walked out of the room.

Fitzwilliam locked the cubicle door and sat down on the closed toilet seat in the cloakroom down the corridor from his boss's office. He looked at his watch — five past four. He sighed. Fifteen minutes. *That's not enough time.*

He took a deep breath and slowly let it out.

What to do?

There was no doubt it was a great career opportunity — a high-profile investigation with direct contact with senior members of the royal family. Those occasions didn't happen often, even within PaIRS. But he loved the intelligence side of his job. He knew he was good at it and was doing well. Couldn't he still climb the ladder as quickly if he stuck to the one discipline? That was the nub of the issue. Copson clearly thought not. She'd said he needed to widen his experience. And of course, he had next to no experience with investigations. Plus, it was only one assignment. It would probably only be for a couple of weeks. How bad could it be?

He sighed. On the whole, he preferred not to deal with people. They rarely told the truth or gave the full picture, and he found that especially frustrating. He wasn't the most patient person in the world, that was for sure. *Will I be able to learn the skills to coax and persuade people into coopera-tion?* What if he screwed it up? How would a bad report from DCI Reed look for his future career? Looking at his watch again, he huffed and raked his hands through his short brown hair. Five minutes left.

And there was Amber to think about. If he ac-cepted this assignment, he would have to cancel their plans to spend time together later this week. He sighed. It was far too early to call her. Neither she nor her family would appreciate being woken up this early in the morning. *If I say yes, surely she will understand this is a once-in-a-lifetime opportu-nity?* And she'd always berated him for choosing Intelligence over Investigation when he'd first joined PaIRS. He blew out his breath. *Who am I kidding?* Amber was so looking forward to their break away together. *There's no way she will be okay with me telling her I can't make it now.* She'd said they needed to reconnect. They could hardly do that if he was on the other side of the country investigating the earl's death.

He stared at the floor. The pattern on the dark-blue vinyl looked like silver rocks embedded in the bottom of the sea. He counted them — one, two, three, four, no, that was a scuff mark, four, five—

His watch beeped. It was nineteen minutes past four. His time had run out.

He stood up, unlocked the door, and stretched first his knees and then his back. They hadn't made these cubicles for a man of six-foot-two to sit in and contemplate his life choices.

Time to talk to Copson.

"Well?" Copson never used ten words when one would do.

"Yes, ma'am, I'd like to work with Reed and his team."

"Good, glad to hear it. I was worried for a minute I'd misread your ambition, Fitzwilliam." She looked up and raised her eyebrows at him.

"No, not at all, ma'am."

"Good." She looked over to the far side of her desk and pulled a piece of paper towards her. "It says here Reed and DS Adler are already on their way to Francis Court. The three of you will oversee the investigation being undertaken by the local Fenshire CID. They will also provide some support resources. You're to be based at Francis Court. No doubt they'll be setting up a temporary office space for you there. You're staying at a hotel in Fawstead, a few miles from Francis-next-the-Sea, which is the village where Francis Court is located." She looked up and shrugged. "That's all I have for you right now. They're expecting you at Francis Court as soon as possible, so I suggest you go home, grab your things, and get on the road. Okay?"

"Yes, ma'am. Do I need to call DCI Reed myself to tell them to expect me?"

"No. I've already told the Super."

Fitzwilliam's eyes opened in surprise. "But I've only this minute told you I would take the job."

"I knew you'd make the right choice, Fitzwilliam." For the first time that morning, Frances Copson smiled. "Now get along with you and do me proud."

14

6:55 AM, WEDNESDAY 4 JANUARY

Fitzwilliam cursed out loud. The traffic piled up ahead of him on the M25 was crawling, and he was getting nowhere fast. He sighed. *I suppose this is normal for seven in the morning.* He was grateful he lived only fifteen minutes from Gollingham Palace and didn't have to deal with a long commute in or around London like this every day. He rolled his shoulders and tried to relax back in his seat. *It will take as long as it takes.* No point in getting wound up about it. He leaned forward and switched on the radio.

"This is the seven o'clock news from the BBC. Reports are coming in that James Wiltshire, the

*Earl of Rossex, was involved in a serious car acci-
dent late last night. We have no further details at
this time but will keep you informed as more information comes in. Now to other news..."*

*Well, it was bound to get out sooner rather than
later.* The press didn't know much yet, only that
he'd been involved in an accident, but it was just a
matter of time before they found out he was dead.
Fitzwilliam jumped slightly when his mobile phone
rang; the screen flashed up with his wife's name.
He pressed the 'accept call' button.

"Good morning, love. You're up early."

"Did you hear the news? The Earl of Rossex
has been involved in a car accident. Mum came in
and woke me. Is it serious?"

Now what do I do? Should he tell his wife the
earl was dead even though a media blackout was in
place? Or should he say nothing and wait until she
found out from the news? *I'll have to tell her.* He
could only imagine how upset she'd be with him if
she knew he'd known and hadn't told her. *I'm
going to be in enough trouble as it is.*

"Darling, are you still there?" she asked.

"Yes, sorry. I'm driving. Yes, I know about the
accident, and yes, it's serious."

"How serious?"

"About as serious as it can get."

She gasped and lowered her voice. "He's dead then?"

"Yes, I'm afraid so. But you're not to tell anyone, Amber. There's a news blackout at the moment, and I shouldn't really be sharing this with you." There was a sniff from the other end of the line. "Are you all right?"

"Yes." She sniffed again. "It's just so sad. He was so young and full of life." She sighed loudly. "He and Lady Beatrice are my favourite royals." She gasped again. "Oh no! She wasn't involved in the accident as well, was she?"

"Not that I know of. It was just him."

"That's a relief. But God, how awful for her. They've only been married a short while." Amber was silent for a few seconds, then there was another sniff.

I should probably say something. She's clearly upset. "Um, yes, it's shocking." That sounded pathetic even to his ears.

"It's more than that, Rich," she cried. "It's a national tragedy. When the truth comes out that he's dead, the public will go nuts and so will the press."

Fitzwilliam had never really understood the public's obsession with the royal family even though he witnessed it every day. He knew she was right. This was going to be a big deal.

There was a sudden change in her voice. "Did you say you were driving, Rich? I thought you'd be in the office by now, especially with all this going on."

Steel yourself... Here goes...

"I'm on my way to Fenshire. I'm on secondment to the team who is overseeing the investigation into the earl's accident." He held his breath as he waited for her to respond.

Her voice was slower and guarded. "Why? You're in Intelligence, not Investigations. Why are you getting involved?"

"Well, they asked—"

She cut in, her voice a few octaves higher than before. "Oh my goodness. This wasn't a normal car accident, was it? It's something terror related. Is that—"

"No," he cried. "Amber, stop. As far as I know, it was a straightforward accident. They've not selected me for my intelligence skills. Copson was asked to recommend a member of her team to be attached to the investigation because one of the regular team is on leave and up a mountain somewhere, so they're a person short. She recommended me."

"Hayden Saunders." Her voice now sounded flat.

"What?" *What is she talking about?*

"Hayden Saunders. He's climbing a mountain in Mexico. I told you about him a few weeks ago. He's the one who got three weeks' leave, remember?"

Fitzwilliam couldn't remember. *Probably not the right time to admit it though.* "Oh yeah," he blurted out. "Anyway, Copson asked me if I would replace him temporarily, and I'm on my way to Francis Court right now. Well, I will be once the traffic gets moving. The M25 is at a standstill. You wouldn't believe the—"

"So you had a choice then?" she cut in.

Oh dear, she sounds as unhappy as I feared she would. "Well, not really, love. She gave me fifteen minutes to decide."

"Why didn't you ring me?" she demanded.

"It was four in the morning." He was trying to keep calm.

"But you hate investigations. You think everyone lies."

She's right, of course. "Copson thinks it will be good for me to push myself out of my comfort zone. Plus, it's a high-profile investigation. My involvement will reflect well on me for my next promotion."

"Of course." Her enunciation was slow and deliberate. "So you won't be back by Friday then?"

"I doubt it, love. Sorry." *I really am sorry, Amber.* Would she believe him?

"So I'll cancel the cottage then, shall I?" she asked, her voice steely and monotone.

What can I say to fix this? "Why don't you go anyway? Have some time on your own away from your family. You can curl up with a good book and go for walks on the beach. It'll be fun." *It sounds great to me.*

"Because I wanted to spend time with you!" she bellowed, her voice shaking.

Fitzwilliam rubbed his forehead. *I've got it wrong again.* He sighed. "I know, and I'm sorry, love. But surely you can understand it's such a great opportunity. I couldn't turn it down."

"You could have done. But clearly your career is more important than us," she spat out.

"That isn't true, and you know it. I'm ultimately doing this for us."

"No, you're not," she cried. "You're doing it for you, Rich!"

"Look, I'm driving right now. I don't think it's the right time to have this conversation. Can we—"

"It never is!" she snapped. The line went dead.

Amber: *I really enjoyed NYE. You make me laugh. Were you serious about taking me out for dinner? x*

Dave: *Of course. I hear that new place on the high street, Marco's, is great. x*

Amber: *Sounds good. I'm free tonight if you are? x*

Dave: *Yes, can't wait. I'll book a table now. See you later. x*

15

MID-MORNING, WEDNESDAY 4 JANUARY

Fitzwilliam pulled off the main road and followed the signs to Francis-next-the-Sea. The country lane with its narrow roads, large green fields on either side, ancient trees, and gnarly hedgerows was bleak and empty. *This really is the middle of nowhere.* His Sat Nav was telling him to turn left, but ahead of him, across the road he was planning to turn onto, was a barrier and a yellow diversion sign. He carried on for a few metres, then pulled off into a lay-by. Checking his Sat Nav again, he was grateful PaIRS had recently paid for their fleet of BMWs to have them installed. The software recalculated the route and told him to carry on and take the next turn left. It would bring him back onto the road he was looking for. He glanced at the clock on his dashboard. It was almost ten. He switched off the CD player and turned on the radio as he pulled out onto the road.

"This is the ten o'clock news from the BBC. Following reports from the Press Association that the Earl of Rossex has died from injuries sustained in a car accident late last night, we are now going live to the press room at Gollingham Palace for a statement."

"Good morning, ladies and gentlemen. It is with deep sadness that their royal highnesses, the King and Queen, have asked for the following announcement to be made immediately.

'Our beloved grandson-in-law, James Wiltshire, the Earl of Rossex, has died following a car accident that took place last night in Fenshire. The earl, who was driving his Audi RS8, was pronounced dead at the scene. Lady Beatrice, the Countess of Rossex, and other members of the royal family, along with the earl's parents, the Earl and Countess of Durrland, have been informed. We currently have no further details and ask the public and the press to respect the privacy of the earl's family at this very difficult time. Thank you.'."

"That was Mr Brian Goody, principle private

secretary to the king, confirming James Wiltshire, the Earl of Rossex, was killed in a car accident last night in Fenshire. We are now going live to our royal correspondent, Jenny Thrift, who is outside Francis Court..."

Fitzwilliam switched down the volume as he turned left. Ten metres ahead of him was a white Ford Mondeo parked in front of a barrier guarded by a uniformed policeman. A second policeman was remonstrating with the car driver. Fitzwilliam slowed down and pulled up behind the car. He walked past the two men and approached the young policeman guarding the entrance to the road.

"I'm sorry, sir, but this road is closed," he informed Fitzwilliam as he walked forward to meet him.

Fitzwilliam removed his ID card from his jacket pocket and showed it to the man. "I'm DS Fitzwilliam from PaIRS. I'm part of the team investigating the earl's accident. They're expecting me at Francis Court, but I'm not able to get there." He smiled, and the young policeman smiled back.

"It's all gone crazy here, sir, what with the press trying to gain access to the estate." He nodded towards the white car, which had now turned around and was heading back down the road. The policeman who'd been talking to the driver was now striding towards them.

"Can we help you, sir?" he shouted as he got closer. *He looks like he's up for another fight.*

"It's okay, sarge," the younger one shouted back, clearly trying to stop his sergeant from making a fool of himself in front of a fellow officer. "This is DS Fitzwilliam."

The sergeant slowed down and raised his hand at Fitzwilliam. He stopped and put his hands on his hips, catching his breath. Fitzwilliam walked up to meet him.

"Hello, sergeant. I was just telling your colleague here that I'm expected at Francis Court, but I can't get through."

The older man nodded. "Well, we can sort it out for you now. I'll radio through to find out where you need to go."

"... we're waiting for further details. The earl was only twenty-four years old, and he married Lady Beatrice, the king's granddaughter, just over a year ago in a lavish ceremony at Fenn House. Since their marriage, the earl and countess have dedi-

cated their lives to public service and are two of the most hard-working younger royals. We believe the accident happened only a few miles from here, and many of the roads in the area are closed off while access to Francis Court is restricted and the accident is investigated."

"And do you know where Lady Beatrice is at present, Jenny?"

"We understand she's on the Francis Court Estate somewhere. The Earl and Countess of Rossex moved into their home, The Dower House, which is on the estate, shortly after their marriage. It's possible, of course, she's up at the main house, where her mother and father live."

"And do we know who else is present at Francis Court at the moment, Jenny?"

"Well, Tom. Lady Sarah Rosdale, the countess's sister, also lives on the estate, and the two sisters are very close. I think we can safely assume she's with her right now. We also believe Her Royal Highness Princess Helen is at Francis Court, although her husband left yesterday to visit Kilkirk House in Ireland. Lady Beatrice's elder brother Lord Fred Astley is not here as he returned to his army unit, based in Colchester, on Monday. The only other resident likely to be currently at Francis Court is Lady Beatrice's paternal *grandmother Olive, the Dowager Countess of Arnwall."*

"Thank you, Jenny. We'll return to you shortly. That was Jenny Thrift, live from Francis Court in Fenshire. Now let's talk to—"

Fitzwilliam switched off the radio as he approached the trade entrance of the Francis Court Estate. He wound down his window and handed over his ID card to the policeman stationed there. A few minutes later, it was returned to him and the barrier lifted. Fitzwilliam drove along the tarmac road, massive rhododendron bushes on either side of him. He shook his head. *I thought there would be more activity.* It was so quiet and peaceful. The sergeant at the first roadblock had told him over a hundred press were already camped out at the main gates and more were expected. As the drive opened up, the colossal stately home of Francis Court lay ahead of him, the morning sun glinting off its many windows. *Wow, that's stunning.* He couldn't imagine what it would be like to live in such an impressive house on a large estate like this. The road twisted to the left, the main house now behind him, and he passed the church, then headed straight towards the striking all-glass Orangery and its attached outbuildings where he'd been told his team was housed. Fitzwilliam swung his car round, scattering gravel, and parked. *Now the fun and games will truly begin.*

"You must be DS Fitzwilliam?" A short stocky man approached him, holding out his hand. "I'm DCI Angus Reed. Welcome to the team." Even if his lilting Scottish accent hadn't given him away, the short red hair and the ginger-toned beard would have been a strong hint of his Gaelic heritage.

Fitzwilliam shook his temporary new boss's hand. "Thank you, sir," he replied as he scanned the room. Four desks set up in a cross formation by the large window on the right-hand side of the room were piled high with phones, computer screens, and boxes with various connectors and wires spewing over the top of them.

"As you can tell, we're not fully set up yet. Fenshire CID has promised me admin support by lunchtime, and their computer geek should be here shortly to get all the electronics working. In the meantime, we're making do as best we can. You'll be in here with DS Adler, who you'll meet shortly. I'm in the office through there." He gestured towards a wooden door at the back of the room. "Fenshire CID are in the two offices next to us, and we have access to a small kitchen that has a hot water boiler and a sink. Adler will give you a proper tour, no doubt." He walked towards his office, then turned back. "I'll give you both a briefing in fifteen minutes." He nodded and walked into his office, closing the door behind him.

Fitzwilliam moved over to the window and sat on a chair in front of the desk with the least amount of debris on it. On the opposite side of the room, an oversized whiteboard was propped up against the wall. A box crammed full of markers, magnets, and string sat next to it on the floor. Fitzwilliam smiled. He'd heard the investigations team still used the old-fashioned method of a board with pictures, words, and notes all linked with red string to make connections and help them untangle alibis and motives. *Maybe I can introduce them to the mind maps and other supporting software we use in Intelligence?* In his opinion, using them was much more efficient.

The door opened, and an attractive woman strolled in. She looked around the room and spotted Fitzwilliam. "Hello," she said as she walked towards him, a huge grin spreading over her face. *What beautiful teeth she has.* Fitzwilliam automatically smiled back. She was petite, maybe five foot plus a little, Fitzwilliam guessed, her thick black hair creating a halo around her smiling oval face. She was dressed in a black suit with a green V-neck T-shirt underneath, the colour complimenting her dark skin tone. *She looks like someone who will be fun to have in the office.*

"Hello back. I'm Richard Fitzwilliam." He rose and held out his hand.

"I'm Emma." She grasped his outstretched hand and shook it firmly. "Have you been shown round yet?"

"No. I'm waiting for DS Adler. He should be here any minute according to the boss." He nodded towards Reed's office. "Would you like me to take you in and introduce you to him? He seems all right from what I've seen so far."

She was no longer smiling.

"Why would you need to do that?" She raised her eyebrows.

What's going on? Had they met already?

"I assumed you haven't been introduced yet as you've only just arrived," he replied, frowning.

"Who do you think I am?" she asked, her head tilted to one side.

"Aren't you the admin support from Fenshire CID?"

She shook her head, glaring at him.

What did I do? One minute, she's smiling, and the next, she's looking at me like it's taking all her willpower not to stab me and leave me for dead.

"I'm sorry. I was told we were expecting an admin person. Oh, hold on. Are you the IT support?" Again, she shook her head. She opened her mouth to speak but was interrupted by Reed's door opening.

"Ah, there you are, Adler. I can see you and DS Fitzwilliam have met already. Good. Right, you'll have to show him around later. I need to give you a briefing before I meet DCI Prior." He waved them into his office.

Aiming a parting look of disgust at Fitzwilliam, Detective Sergeant Emma Adler followed her boss into his office.

Fitzwilliam slapped his hand to his forehead. *Well, that couldn't have gone much worse.*

16

SHORTLY AFTER, WEDNESDAY 4 JANUARY

Statement from Fenshire police:
We are asking for witnesses who were driving in the Fenshire area within a ten-mile radius of Francis-next-the-Sea between the hours of 9:00 pm on Tuesday 3 Jan and 1:00 am on Wednesday 4 Jan, to get in contact with Fenshire CID on the number on our website.

"So we have a complication." Reed was propped up against the front of his desk, his arms folded, his backside resting on the top of the table. "There was a woman passenger in the earl's car. She was alive when the emergency services arrived, but she died not long after they admitted her to hospital. She has been identified as Gill Sterling, wife of Alex Sterling, the estate manager here at Francis Court."

"Do we know what she was doing in the car with the earl?" Adler stood to the left of Fitzwilliam, her notebook in her right hand, her left busily scribbling. She hadn't looked at Fitzwilliam since they'd entered the room.

Reed shook his head. "No. Neither do we have any idea why the earl was in this area last night. He was due to be staying at Knightsbridge Court overnight." He turned towards Fitzwilliam. "How much do you know about the case so far, Fitzwilliam?"

"Not much, sir. All I was told by DCI Copson was that the Earl of Rossex had been killed in a car accident late last night. And, of course, I've heard what the news has been reporting on the way here."

Reed tugged at his beard. "The media blackout was broken at seven when the French got wind of the story. I assume you heard the statement made by Gollingham Palace?"

Fitzwilliam nodded.

"Adler can fill you in on the details after this meeting. But briefly, what we know so far is that the earl's Audi came off the road last night and ploughed into a tree. The car was found by a local couple on their way back from having dinner with some friends at around twelve-thirty, and they called the emergency services. There was an initial statement taken from them by the police on-site. The earl was pronounced dead at the scene, and Mrs Sterling was still alive at that point. Fenshire CID will collate any information that comes in following our appeal for witnesses."

He turned round and scooped a piece of paper from his desk. "The Countess of Rossex Lady Beatrice is with her mother Her Royal Highness Princess Helen and her sister Lady Sarah Rosdale at The Dower House, which is here on the estate. Our point of contact for them at the moment is a chap called" —he referred to the paper in his hand— "Rory Glover. He's the earl and countess's private secretary. I have requested an interview with Lady Beatrice, but I don't expect my request will be granted today."

Why not? Surely talking to her was a priority. He looked over at Adler. It was hard to gauge her reaction as she was still ignoring him, but she didn't seem put out by Reed's statement that it was unlikely they would be able to interview the countess today. *Maybe that's normal for an investigation involving the royal family?* This was all new to him, and he was keen to ask questions. However, he was also conscious of the fact that Reed wasn't necessarily aware of his lack of experience. *Maybe it would be better to just watch and listen for now.* Adler was waiting, her pen poised. *I don't want to make even more of a fool of myself than I have already.*

"So our job is to make sure this incident was an accident and to ensure there is no threat to any other members of the royal family." Reed dropped the paper back on his desk.

Adler raised her hand. "Is there any question of it *not* being an accident, sir?"

"On the face of it, no. It appears to be straightforward. But we need to work with local CID to establish the earl's movements prior to the accident, review the reports from forensics, scene of crime, and witnesses, and make sure nothing needs following up or is inconsistent with what we know." He lifted himself off the desk. "Right, I'm off to a meeting with DCI Prior." He turned to Fitzwilliam. "DCI Matt Prior is from Fenshire CID and leading the investigation at their end. We will be working with him and his team. They will do most of the donkey work with the help of the local uniform boys. In terms of witness statements and the like, we will deal with any aspects that require contact with the royal family." He looked at his watch.

"Right, I really need to go. Adler, can you show Fitzwilliam around and fill him in on anything I've missed?"

Still not acknowledging Fitzwilliam, she gave a curt nod.

"After that, please interview Mr Glover and find out the earl's movements leading up to the accident." He turned to look directly at Fitzwilliam. "I'd like you to interview Mr and Mrs Maynard. They were first on the scene." He walked around to the front of the desk and picked up his mobile phone and a piece of paper. "Here is their statement taken by the local police." He handed the paper to Fitzwilliam. "We'll meet again at four for an update briefing. Thank you both." He swept out of the room.

Adler, without looking back at Fitzwilliam, followed him out.

"Look, I'm sorry I mistook you for the admin person," Fitzwilliam said as he walked back into the outer office. Adler was at the desk by the window in front of her laptop, reading.

She looked up and scowled at him. "And why did you think that, detective sergeant?" She didn't give him time to reply. "Is it because I'm a woman?" Her large brown eyes fixed on him.

Fitzwilliam swallowed. *Is there anything I can say to fix this? Or will I just make it worse?* "No, I can assure you. I really am sorry. I was led to believe DS Adler was a man."

"Led to believe? Or assumed?" Her stare unnerved him. Heat rose up his neck. He looked down at his feet. *I could have sworn Reed referred to Adler as 'he'. There are so few women in PaIRS… So could she be right? Did I just assume Adler would be a man?*

"I honestly don't know." He shook his head and waited for the roasting to continue. *I deserve it.*

She sighed and closed her laptop. "Well, at least you're honest about it." She rose from the desk and held out her hand. "Let's start again, shall we? Hello, I'm Detective Sergeant Emma Adler."

Fitzwilliam smiled and took her hand. "Hello, Detective Sergeant Emma Adler. I'm Detective Sergeant Richard Fitzwilliam, and as you can probably tell, I'm not great with people."

She laughed and shook his hand.

"So how did you end up here, Fitzwilliam? Aren't you an Intelligence guy?" Adler handed him one of the two cups of coffee she was carrying, then walked to her desk and sat opposite him.

"Thank you." He looked up from the witness statement he had been reading.

"You're welcome. But just so we're clear, it's your turn to make me the tea next time."

He nodded and smiled. "My boss recommended me. Reed was looking for someone to come and replace one of your team who's on leave."

"Yes. Saunders' up a mountain in Mexico at the moment, the idiot. Serves him right for doing something so daft. He'll be kicking himself when he finds out he's missing this." She chuckled. "So why you, though? If you're not good with people, I'm surprised they selected you. After all, investigation is ninety percent dealing with people one way or another."

Fitzwilliam sighed. "I know, but she thinks if I want to progress in the organisation, I need to round out my experience, and this is a great opportunity to do that."

She nodded. "Well, they've definitely thrown you in at the deep end."

"What's Reed like to work for?" He was keen to know more about his temporary boss. After all, the report he got from Reed at the end of this assignment could be critical to his future.

"He's all right. I've been with him for six months now, and he treats me like any other member of the team. Which is a big deal for me. So for that alone, he gets my vote."

Fitzwilliam raised his eyebrows. "What do you mean when you say he treats you like any other member of the team? Why shouldn't he?"

She smiled. "That's rich coming from the man who assumed I was the admin help."

Fitzwilliam blushed. "I'm so sorry."

She was still smiling. "Don't sweat it." Her smile faded. "But it's tough being a woman in PaIRS. Do you know how many of us there are?" Fitzwilliam shook his head. "Eight. That's in the whole organisation. And your boss, Frances Copson, is the most senior of us all. And I'm one of only two black female officers."

Fitzwilliam's eyes widened. "I knew PaIRS was male dominated, but I had no idea it was that bad. I was in City until last year, and there are plenty of senior female officers. My wife's a DS there."

"City is different. There are more women, especially following the recent recruitment campaign they did targeting us. And there are more black officers anyway because of the demographics of London. But PaIRS is much harder to get into. Didn't you find that?"

"Not really. I got offered a position in PaIRS shortly after they promoted me to sergeant."

"Ah, well, there you are. A young, ambitious, white man. I bet you're middle class too. You tick all the usual boxes."

"Actually, after my dad left us with no money, we lived in a council house in one of the roughest areas of Leeds for a while. So you can definitely strike middle class off your list."

She studied him, her head to one side.

I'm not sure she believes me. "So what made you join PaIRS then?"

"I like a challenge." She grinned, then continued, "I'm also female, black, and a single parent. Oh, *and* I'm gay. I'm the golden ticket when it comes to diversity, so they jumped at the chance to get me on board." She laughed.

Now he was the one who was unsure if he believed her. "So you have a child then?"

"Yes, I have a thirteen-year-old daughter. We live with my parents, and they look after her when I'm away." She rose and picked up her laptop, sliding it into its cover and placing it in a large leather bag, which she pulled up onto her shoulder. "Well, it's been great chatting, but I have an appointment to meet Mr Glover, and I don't want to be late."

Fitzwilliam picked up his phone and rose from his desk. "And I need to see our star witnesses."

She looked back over her shoulder. "They've had a tremendous shock. Be nice to them."

17

MIDDAY, WEDNESDAY 4 JANUARY

"Would you like a cup of coffee or tea, sergeant?" Kim Maynard led him along the wide and airy hall and into a large bright living room.

"Coffee would be great, Mrs Maynard, if it's not too much trouble."

"No, not at all." She smiled at him, and her face softened. *She looks tired*, Fitzwilliam thought. *Adler is right. This must be a huge shock for them. I'll be extra nice.*

A tall man in his fifties got up from a leather Chesterfield sofa as they entered and held out his hand.

His wife introduced them. "This is my husband, Terry. Terry, this is Detective Sergeant Fitzwilliam." Fitzwilliam took the offered hand and shook it.

"Thank you for taking the time to talk to me, Mr Maynard. This must be an unpleasant shock for you both."

Terry waved him towards a green armchair opposite the sofa. He glanced at the door his wife had disappeared through and said softly, "Kim is finding it particularly hard. The telephone has been ringing off the hook, until we literally took it off the hook. The press was gathered outside earlier. They were knocking on the door and shouting through the letterbox. Kim was very upset. Fortunately, the local police came and dispersed them an hour ago." He glanced at the door again and whispered, "Kim told her sister early this morning what happened, and she's such a blabbermouth. I think it was her who told the press—" He stopped abruptly as his wife entered, carrying a large tray.

Fitzwilliam immediately rose and, taking the tray from her, placed it on the coffee table.

"Thank you, sergeant." Her eyes shone with tears.

Oh no, did I get it wrong already?

She wiped the side of one eye, then bent forward over the tray. They sat in silence while she poured and distributed the hot drinks. When she finished, she sat next to her husband on the sofa and smiled across at Fitzwilliam.

"I know you both gave a brief statement to the local police early this morning," he began. They nodded. "I've read your statements, and I don't think it's necessary for you to repeat to me what you've already told them." Kim's shoulders relaxed, and she let her head fall back onto the sofa. Terry reached across and took his wife's hand. She turned and smiled at him.

"What I'd like to do, if it's all right with you, is ask you some questions that will expand on your statement." Terry nodded and squeezed his wife's hand. She sat back up and picked up her tea with her free hand.

Fitzwilliam got out his notebook, where he'd already jotted down the questions he wanted to ask, and took out his pen.

"What time did you leave here to visit your friends?"

Kim put down her cup. "It would have been about seven-twenty. It's less than ten minutes away."

"Thank you. Did you see or pass any other cars on your way there?"

She looked at her husband. "I don't think so. Do you, darling?"

Terry shook his head. "No, the road was deserted. Just us."

Fitzwilliam made a note in his notebook and looked at the next question. "What about on the way back from your friends? You left them at about twelve-thirty, I believe. Did you see any other cars?"

They both shook their heads.

"All we saw before we got to the scene of the accident was a large deer. He gave me a bit of a shock, I can tell you. We came round the bend and discovered him in the middle of the road." Terry looked at his wife, and she nodded.

"They're everywhere this time of year, sergeant," she told him. "They're solitary animals a lot of the year, but in the winter, they make up groups and move around together. We're used to it, I guess, and tend to take it easy on these roads."

Her husband looked down at his shoes.

"Thank you. That's very helpful." It wasn't really, but Fitzwilliam was trying to make them feel at ease. "So next, can I ask you about when you found the car?" He referred to his notes. "It was you, Mr Maynard, who got to the car first?"

"Yes. Kim rang the emergency services, and I went to see if there was anything I could do. I'm ex-Army and have had some combat first aid training, so I thought I may be able to help."

Fitzwilliam smiled at him. "Who were you with, Mr Maynard?"

Terry Maynard sat up straight. "East Anglian Rifles, sergeant. I left five years ago after thirty years."

"I was Army Air Corps myself. I only did ten years though."

"Best years of my life," the older man said.

Fitzwilliam nodded. "So when you got to the car, Mr May—"

"Call me Terry, please."

"Okay, Terry. When you got to the car, what did you do first?"

"Well, I went to the driver's side, but it had taken the brunt of the impact, and I could see straight away I wasn't going to get to the driver that way, so I ran around the back of the car to the passenger door—"

"Was it open or shut, Terry?"

Terry Maynard paused, his head leaning slightly to one side. "Well, I don't quite know. I had to pull the door away from the frame to gain access. It opened easily. It wasn't stuck or anything. I didn't think about it back then, but I'm surprised I didn't have to really yank it to get it open." A frown creased his forehead.

Fitzwilliam made a note in his book. "Not to

worry, Terry. The impact may have forced it open. So what did you do next?"

"I looked inside to assess the situation." He paused and leaned down to touch the teapot in front of him. He turned to his wife. "Kim, love, can you top up the pot with some hot water, please?"

"Of course." She rose and, picking up the teapot, carried it out of the room.

"Sorry about that, sergeant, but I don't want to upset her. I've seen enough injuries and death to not be fazed by it, but my wife hasn't, thank goodness."

Fitzwilliam nodded.

"Anyway, I realised from the position he was in and the colour of him that the driver was dead. I did lean over and check for a pulse, but—" He shook his head.

"And the passenger?" Fitzwilliam asked.

"I couldn't tell by looking at her, so I checked for a pulse. She was at an awkward angle so it was hard to find the right spot. It took me a good few minutes before I got a faint one."

"And what position was she in, Terry?"

"She was twisted over in her seat, her head resting on the dash."

"And the driver?"

"His head was on the steering wheel, which had

been pushed up and inwards from the force of the crash."

"Could you see if they both had seat belts on?"

"Yes, they were both still strapped in. The air bags had gone off, although by then, they'd deflated."

"Thank you, Terry," Fitzwilliam said as he jotted down what he'd been told.

Kim walked back into the room and placed the teapot on the table. She glanced at her husband, and he nodded at her. She sat down and crossed her hands in her lap.

"You'll be pleased to hear I'm almost done," Fitzwilliam said, smiling at them. "It said in your statement you stayed with the female passenger until the emergency services arrived. Did she regain consciousness during that time?"

They shook their heads.

"And you covered her with a coat, I believe. Where did you get that from?"

To his surprise, Kim answered. "The lady who took the emergency call stayed on the line with me. She was so calm. She asked if there was anything we could put over the passenger to keep her warm. She said not to use the coats we were wearing as she didn't want us to get cold and be ill. When we said we didn't have anything, she suggested we looked in the crashed car's boot, so while Terry was giving her an update on the woman's condition, I went and found a coat, and Terry used it to cover her up."

"And when you went to the boot of the car, was it shut?"

She paused and frowned. "Now you mention it, I don't think it was. I didn't have to press anything to release a catch. It just pulled up. Does that mean it was open already, sergeant?"

Fitzwilliam was busy scribbling and didn't answer immediately. Mrs Maynard waited, her hands in her lap, and watched him write.

"Sorry," he said as he looked up. "It's possible the catch popped open when the car hit the tree. I'm sure it's not unusual, but we'll get Forensics to have a look at it anyway. And did you notice what else was in the boot, Mrs Maynard?"

"There was a black case. You know, the overnight size with wheels and a pull-up handle. I didn't see anything else. I was more interested in grabbing the coat and taking it to Terry."

"Of course. I don't expect you noticed if the case was open or closed?"

"I don't know. Let me think." Kim raised her hands to her forehead and closed her eyes.

Fitzwilliam took a sip of his coffee.

"The top zips weren't quite closed. There was a gap of maybe this much" —she lowered her hands and held her fingers seven centimetres apart— "between them. I remember now as I could see something white poking out of the opening." She looked up at Fitzwilliam and shrugged.

That's interesting. I wonder why it was open? He nodded and smiled. "Thank you, Mrs Maynard. That's very helpful." He slipped his pocketbook into the inside of his jacket and rose. "That's all I need to ask you at this stage. Once again, thank you for your co-operation in this matter."

Terry and Kim rose in unison, smiling back.

"We're glad to be of help," Terry told him as he extended his hand. Fitzwilliam returned the handshake.

"And thank you for my coffee," he said to Kim as they walked down the hall. "If you have any more trouble with the press, please give me a ring and I will do what I can to help." He handed her his card.

I think I was very nice, he congratulated himself as he walked to his car.

18

ALSO MID-DAY, WEDNESDAY 4 JANUARY

"—so if you can go through all the calls we've had and collate them please, Lattimore. I have a meeting now in King's Town and then I'll be back here later for an update with the PaIRS guys." Detective Chief Inspector Matt Prior rubbed his shovel-like hands together as he addressed a stocky young man in a striped shirt and chinos.

"Yes, sir." Detective Constable Simon Lattimore placed his mug of tea on the table by the pile of papers and walked around the desk to sit down.

"Great. I'll see you later." The lofty chief inspector bent down as he exited through the door.

I bet he's only going back to the office because it's warmer there.

Lattimore picked up his steaming mug of tea

and wrapped his hands around the hot vessel. He blew on the liquid, then took a sip. *I'll try to nick one of those portable heaters from the office when I'm back in King's Town and bring it here.*

He relished the feeling of the hot tea slipping down his throat as he looked out the window to the side of him. The sun was just poking through the clouds, radiating out its orange light in a semi-circle above them. Simon smiled to himself as he watched a kestrel hover by a tree, its shape silhouetted in front of the white sky. *I can't believe I'm here, sitting in an office at Francis Court, part of the most high-profile investigation we've ever had in Fenshire.*

He put down his mug and gathered the car sighting reports in front of him, smoothing each one down and finally piling them up. Picking up the first one, he reviewed it. As he meticulously studied each report, he extracted the key information and corresponding times and matched them to the sighting, recording it on a spreadsheet on his laptop.

At the end of the process, he had two reports that looked interesting. He looked at the first one again. A local couple had seen a black Range Rover with its hazard lights on, sat on the side of the same road where the accident had happened at approximately ten past eleven. As they had passed the vehicle, the passenger had looked over to see if anyone had needed help and had seen two men. The driver had been on his phone. The witnesses had thought they might have broken down, but they'd looked like they'd had it all under control, so the couple had carried on home, which was just around the next corner. They hadn't gone as far as the accident site.

The second lead was from a visitor to the area who had been returning to his rented holiday cottage. He'd reported he'd just turned onto the road from the other end as the first lead at about twenty past eleven, when two vehicles had rushed past him. He'd said they had been travelling close to each other, tailgating almost dangerously. One had been a black Range Rover, and it had been following a black estate car. Again, the witness had pulled off the road towards where he was staying shortly after the sighting and hadn't gone as far as the accident site.

Simon did a last check of the schedule he'd produced. *No, I'm right. Neither of those two vehicles have come forward to say they were in the area.*

Simon opened a word processing document and started to type: *1) Was the Range Rover seen by the couple the same one the man saw ten minutes later?* He went back to the witness statements. Neither had been able to give a registration number for the vehicles they'd seen. *But hold on.* He referred to them both at the same time. The woman in the first car had reported that the number plate had looked 'odd' and 'not like a regular UK plate'. The witness in the other car had said that the plate had looked 'foreign,' but he hadn't been able to be more specific. That would suggest they'd both seen the same Range Rover. He continued: *2) Assuming they are the same, then if the RR and estate car were tailgating each other why did it take the RR ten minutes to drive that stretch of road?; 3) Or had the RR broken down and the second car come to help?; 4) If so, did they drive past the earl's car before or after the accident? Note: Ring Roisin re estimated time of accident; 5) Why haven't the drivers come forward? Note: put out an appeal for the specific cars?; 6) Could the RR have been a lookout?*

Simon chuckled to himself and deleted the last item. He was being 'fanciful', as his fiancée Sharron liked to call it.

He picked up his mobile and dialled Roisin at Forensics at Fenshire HQ in King's Town.

"Hey, Si. What are you up to?" Her gentle Irish accent always made Simon feel calmer and more relaxed.

"Hey, Ro. You won't believe it, I'm at Francis

Court, and" —he leaned his face against the window and twisted his head to the right— "I have the most amazing view of the Orangery here. It's just beautiful."

"Well, check you out, Mr-I-only-work-in-the-poshest-places. Are you on the earl's accident investigation then?"

"Yes. How lucky am I? My second assignment since I joined CID, and I've landed a big one."

"You're not kidding. Everyone here is running around like headless chickens trying to get the accident scene stuff processed double quick."

"I can imagine. I have a quick question. Does anyone have a more accurate time of accident than between nine and twelve-thirty yet?"

"Funny you should ask that. My boss was just discussing it with DCI Prior. They've narrowed it down to between eleven and eleven-thirty."

Simon made a note on his laptop. "How come?"

"They can tell from the injuries, especially from the woman who was still alive when they arrived on the scene."

"Great, thanks, Ro. That helps me a lot."

"Will you be back at HQ today?"

"I doubt it, but I'll see you later at home," he told his housemate.

"Aren't you seeing Sharron tonight?"

"No. They have a parents' evening and then she's going out for a meal with some of the other teachers."

"Cool, I'll see you later then. Text me when you're leaving, and I'll order a Chinese takeaway."

"Perfect. See you later."

Simon put his mobile phone down on the table and added to his list: *6) If TOA is between eleven and eleven-thirty, then these two vehicles might have seen something.*

19

LATE AFTERNOON, WEDNESDAY 4 JANUARY

"So what do we have?" Reed asked as he looked around the room.

Fitzwilliam tried to move closer to the window to grab some of the fresh air the gap in it provided. *This office is way too small to do a briefing in!* Taking a gulp of air, he scanned the small office. Aside from himself and Adler, he knew the large-framed man standing next to Reed. That was Prior, who Reed had introduced to him and Adler before the meeting had started. The other two men were unknown to him. One was tall and scruffy. Most likely CID. He stood next to Prior. So probably his DS. The other man was in uniform, his rank slides confirming he was an inspector. *Fenshire uniform branch*, Fitzwilliam guessed.

"Adler. Do you want to go first?"

Adler opened her pocketbook. "I interviewed Mr Rory Glover, private secretary to the Earl and Countess of Rossex. He confirmed the countess had no appointments for yesterday or today as she is recovering from a sickness bug. The earl had gone to London on Tuesday to attend a charity committee meeting at three in the afternoon. He was due to stay in London overnight at Knightsbridge Court where the earl and countess have a grace-and-favour apartment for their use when they're in the capital. He had private errands scheduled for this morning and was due back this afternoon. The earl and countess had public duty appointments for the rest of this week, which, of course, Glover has cancelled.

"With regards to security, the earl only had police protection when he was performing public duties. The earl drove himself to London yesterday morning, accompanied by his brother-in-law Lord Frederick Astley, who was returning to his military unit based in Central London. They had a police escort. A PaIRS protection detail accompanied the earl to his charity meeting, and when it finished at five, they returned to Knightsbridge Court. The earl rang Glover at five-thirty to have an end-of-day catchup, and he told Glover he was going to speak to his wife next. The earl had the evening free, and as far as Glover knows, he had no plans. Glover is clearly upset but keeping a stiff upper lip." She closed her notebook and looked over at Reed perched on the top of his desk, his arms crossed.

"Thank you, Adler. Fitzwilliam, can you tell us how you got on interviewing the first witnesses on the scene — the Maynards?"

Fitzwilliam opened his mouth, but before he could get a word out, Reed said, "I'm only interested in anything additional to their initial statement, which we've all read." He nodded to the uniformed policeman, who nodded back.

"Yes, of course. So there are only three things of note. First, the front passenger door may have been open when the Maynards arrived. Second, the boot was most likely also open when they got on the scene, and finally, Mrs Sterling's bag, which was in the boot, was partially unzipped."

"Why do you think any of that is relevant to the investigation, sergeant?" Prior shuffled around so his six-foot-four body faced Fitzwilliam.

"I'm not sure, sir, but I feel they're worth a closer look in conjunction with the accident scene report."

Reed turned to Prior. "It's worth looking into, I think, Matt," he said before turning back to

Fitzwilliam. "But remember, Fitzwilliam, we're only interested in facts that can be supported by evidence, not the may-have-beens suggested by a witness. With royal cases, it's not uncommon for witnesses to lie just to get their fifteen minutes of fame."

"Yes, sir."

"Matt, do you have anything new from your team?"

"Forensics have narrowed down the time of death to between eleven and eleven-thirty. One of my detectives is collating the calls we've had in following the appeal for drivers in the area on Tuesday evening. Anything further on that, Turner?"

"Lattimore should have the report completed in the next hour, sir. I will send a copy out to everyone in this room. He's proposing we put out a specific appeal for two vehicles that were seen around the time of the accident but haven't come forward yet." The tall, scruffy man, now identified as Turner, turned towards the two chief inspectors. "Are you okay for us to do that?"

Reed frowned. "I want to see the report first and then get one of my team to speak to the witnesses who saw these cars before we do anything else. The drivers may come forward themselves, it's early days. To be honest, I'm not keen to make another appeal via the press at the moment. It will only cause further speculation. But yes, if we need to, then we will."

"I agree," added Prior. "Let's see Lattimore's report first, sergeant, and we'll go from there."

Turner nodded. "Then that's all from me, sir."

"Inspector, anything from you?" He directed the question to the uniformed policeman, who shook his head in response.

"Thank you, everyone. I'll just add that the Countess of Rossex has agreed to see me at ten to-morrow morning at The Dower House. Fitzwilliam, you'll come with me. Princess Helen insists on being present to support her daughter. Unusual, I know, but I could hardly refuse." He grunted. "Matt, I'll catch up with you later. Inspector, thanks for your attendance. Adler and Fitzwilliam, will you stay behind, please?"

Fitzwilliam was relieved when the others left, leaving the room less crowded. He took a deep breath in and, glancing around the room, caught Adler's eye. She too was taking a deep breath. They smiled at each other.

Reed shut the door. "Right, I know it's been a long day. We've all been working for over eighteen hours already, and I don't believe anyone is productive after so long. I want you to call it a day now. I understand you're both staying locally?" They nodded. "Good. So go to your hotel now, eat, and get some rest. In the morning, Adler, I want you to contact the PaIRS protection team at Knightsbridge Court and get their statements about the earl's movements while they were with him. Fitzwilliam, can you look at the report about the car sightings when it gets here and see if any of the witnesses are worth talking to to find out more information about these cars? I'm off to King's Town for a meeting with Forensics. I'll let you know what comes out of that tomorrow. See you both bright and early in the morning."

Fitzwilliam threw his mobile phone on the bed. *Where the heck are you, Amber?*

Storming across the hotel room, he plonked himself into a navy-blue armchair by the window. He'd been trying to get hold of his wife all day and now could only conclude she was deliberately avoiding him. *What can I do? I can't fix this if she won't talk to me!*

He slowly stretched his head to the side, trying to dispel the stiffness in his neck. He sighed. One last try and then he'd give up for now and have a bath. He walked over and retrieved his phone from on top of the blue woollen blanket, draped casually but oh so carefully over the end of the bed.

He dialled a number and waited.

"Hello, Richard. How are you?" The female's voice at the other end of the line sounded nervous.

What's going on?

"I'm fine thanks, Moira. Is Amber there? I can't seem to get hold of her on her mobile."

His mother-in-law hesitated, then huffed. "Er, silly girl. She must have gone out and left it in her room by mistake." She gave an unconvincing laugh.

Fitzwilliam pinched his lips together. "So she's out then, is she?"

"Yes, she's gone to the cinema with some friends, I believe. Can I take a message?"

He felt like a young lad again, having to leave a message for his girlfriend with her parents. *It's so embarrassing!* "If you could ask her to call me when she's back, that would be great."

He wanted to get off this awkward call as soon as he could.

"Of course, Richard."

"Thanks, Moira. Take care."

He cut the call and dropped the phone onto one

of the bedside tables, then yanked his case up onto the bed.

Well, there's nothing else I can do. She clearly doesn't want to talk to me. I don't believe for one minute she's forgotten her phone. She's never without it! Well, she can sulk all she wants. I have a job to do.

Fitzwilliam padded out of the bathroom and across to the bed. The hotel robe wrapped tightly around him, he felt languid, and the gigantic bed before him was calling his name. He drew back the white duvet and sat down on the edge of the bed, picking up his phone to check if Amber had rung or texted. Nothing. He fell back onto the bed and stared up at the ceiling. *I'm overreacting because I'm tired. I need to sleep.* He pulled himself back up, took off his robe, and got into bed. He switched off the light, and letting out a deep breath, he closed his eyes.

Why did the earl go back to Francis Court? He didn't seem to have plans to do so and no one we know of was expecting him.

His brain hadn't got the message it was time to rest.

He opened his eyes, switched on the bedside light, and picked up his mobile phone.

Fitz: *When you interviewed the earl's PS, did he say how the earl was when he'd spoken to him? Did he sound normal?*

Adler: *And this can't wait until the morning because? I wouldn't have given you my number if I'd known you are one of those people who can't switch off from work!*

Fitz: *I find a brain dump at the end of each day helps me sleep.*

Adler: *Weirdo!*

Fitz: *Are you going to answer my question or insult me?*

Adler: *Can I do both?*

. . .

Fitz: *Oh no, are you one of those people who can multitask?*

Adler: *Touche! Glover said the earl sounded perfectly normal to him, and the last thing he'd said was he would ring him the next morning before he left to travel back.*

Fitz: *And did he say what the private errands were the earl needed to do the next morning?*

Adler: *He didn't know. The earl has access to his own diary online to add private commitments, and he'd added an entry that just said 'private errands'. Glover didn't ask him what they were. He said it was none of his business.*

Fitz: *Hopefully Lady Rossex can throw some light on it tomorrow.*

. . .

Adler: *Any more annoying questions to stop me from going to sleep?*

Fitz: *No.*

Fitz: *Oh hang on, yes! Do you think there could be more to this than a straightforward car accident?*

Adler: *Nothing so far makes me think that.*

Fitz: *The open car door and boot, plus her case not closed. It all seems strange to me...*

Adler: *Based on what? The car was in a huge smash!*

Fitz: *I know. It's just a feeling.*

Adler: *Oh no, not a feeling! They're dangerous in investigations. And just to warn you, Reed isn't in-*

terested in thoughts or feelings, only what you know and can prove. Good night...

20

8:00 AM, THURSDAY 5 JANUARY

"So have you seen Ellie yet?" Perry Juke, Francis Court tour guide, tilted his blond head to one side and eyed up his breakfast companion.

"No. I've only spoken to her. She rang to say she wouldn't be in for a few days." Claire Beck, from Human Resources, mirrored Perry's head tilt, her full lips down turned.

Come on, Claire, you can do better than that!

"And? How did she sound?" His blue eyes shone with excitement.

"Dreadful. She could—" She shook her head at Perry as the server reached them. Placing two coffees in front of them, the server told them their food would be with them soon and retreated.

"Go on," Perry urged.

"She could hardly keep it together. I thought she would burst into tears at any minute." Claire pushed her red glasses further up her nose.

Poor Ellie Gunn!

"Really? Oh poor love." He nodded gravely and picked up his coffee. "Although I don't get why she's quite so upset. She didn't really like Gill."

Claire leaned in. "Alex Sterling isn't talking to her. I think he's ended it."

"No!" Perry cried much louder than he'd intended. He looked around the room, his eyes wide. Fortunately, the restaurant wasn't busy yet, just a handful of staff eating. One perk of working at Francis Court was the free breakfast and lunch provided.

"She must be devastated," he whispered. Claire nodded.

"Although, can you really blame him?" he continued. "His wife has just died — I suppose it's embarrassing to have a girlfriend hanging off your arm in the circumstances."

Claire reached over and playfully slapped Perry's arm. "Come on, not everyone knows Ellie and Alex are an item. They could have just kept a low profile until it all blew over."

She's right. A short while of not seeing each

other in public would have been enough. So why end it with Ellie?

"Guilt!" Perry said, his eyebrows shooting up. "I bet he feels guilty, and that's why he's cut Ellie off."

Claire pursed her lips. "I think you've hit the nail on the head. He feels bad he was cheating on his wife."

They looked around as the door opened and a young man wearing chinos and a blue striped shirt entered. *He's hot!* Perry's eyes opened wide as he watched the stocky man with short brown hair cross the room.

"He's not staff," Claire said, smoothing down her honey-blonde hair. "I wonder what he's doing in here?"

Get your paws off, Claire. I saw him first! "No idea, but I'm not complaining." He grinned at her, a twinkle in his eyes, and she laughed.

Simon Lattimore stopped just beyond the door of the restaurant and scanned the room for a quiet table where he could wait. Spotting one in the far corner, he headed towards it just as the server came out of the kitchen, carrying a tray ladened with food and cutlery. On a trajectory that would end in a messy disaster if one of them didn't change their course, they stopped just short of each other and stepped aside in unison, expecting the other to pass on the opposite side. Except it didn't happen. Instead, they mirrored each other's movements. Twice. After what felt like an embarrassingly long time to Simon, he stood still and allowed the server to go around him. Red-faced, he looked down, the giggling from a table behind following him as he scuttled off towards the corner of the room.

"Shush, he'll hear you." Perry glared at Claire.

"Sorry, but it was such a cute little dance."

Perry looked over to where the man now sat. *He looks so embarrassed. I hope he didn't hear Claire laughing.* The man turned his face towards Perry, and large brown eyes stared back at him. Perry was aware of a fluttering sensation in his stomach. He smiled at the handsome stranger. The man smiled back.

"Did you hear me?" Claire's voice made Perry jump.

He reluctantly tore his gaze away from the attractive man, and he turned back to Claire. "No, sorry, what did you say?"

"I said, I wonder what Gill Sterling was doing in the earl's car, anyway."

"Well, yes, I think that's the question everyone is asking. I didn't even know they knew one another, did you?"

Claire shook her head. She leaned in. "I heard the earl wasn't even supposed to be here on Tuesday night. He was meant to be up in London and not due back until yesterday afternoon."

"Well, that's strange then," Perry agreed as the server reached them. She placed their food in front of them. "Anything else?" she asked as she placed the cutlery wrapped in serviettes on the table.

"No, thank you, we're good," Claire replied, unravelling her knife and fork. "So what do you think?" she asked Perry, digging into her scrambled egg on muffins.

Perry shook his head. "I've no idea. I didn't really know Gill well. Although I heard she wasn't very friendly and was always complaining about Alex working all the time."

"She wasn't happy about moving from Drew Castle, where they were before, I believe. Mrs C and Ellie asked her to join them for coffee a couple of times, but she didn't seem to want to make friends with anyone here." Claire put her knife down to pick up her coffee cup before continuing, "As for the earl, I rarely saw him about the place these days since him and Lady Beatrice moved into The Dower House."

"Has anyone seen her?" Perry asked through a mouthful of French toast.

"Lady Beatrice?"

Perry nodded.

"No. Lady Sarah called the boss yesterday to say she wouldn't be around for a few days. But that's all I know. Poor Lady Beatrice, losing her husband and with them only married a short while."

Perry wiped his mouth and laid down his napkin. "I know she can be a bit stuck-up, but you wouldn't wish that on anyone, would you?"

Claire shook her head as she pushed her plate away. "Especially not when your husband is found in the car with another woman!"

———

"Did you get hold of your wife last night?" Adler squinted as she shielded her eyes from the glare of the low sun streaming through the window.

Fitzwilliam shook his head as he got up from his desk. Walking over to the window, he pulled the blind down. "Better?" She smiled and nodded. "She was out according to her mother and had forgotten her phone."

She tilted her head to one side. "But you're not so sure?"

Amber doesn't go anywhere without her phone. And why didn't she ring when she got back from the cinema?

He sat down again and folded his arms across his chest. "I think she's still mad at me and making sure I know it."

In an out-of-character move, Fitzwilliam had told Adler over a quick pub dinner last night about his wife's overreaction to his taking the role within investigations. Not one who naturally shared his personal issues with work colleagues, he'd been surprised at how easy Adler had been to talk to.

She nodded. "Give her a few days. I'm sure she'll come around." She glanced at her watch. "Reed is late."

"So any idea what this special briefing is all about?" Fitzwilliam asked.

"No idea. But I wonder if it's something to do with why Mrs Sterling was in the car. Maybe they've found out something about their relationship?"

Fitzwilliam frowned. "You think she and the earl were having an affair?"

"Don't you?"

Fitzwilliam shrugged. "I haven't really thought about it, to be honest." He grinned at her. "Anyway, what happened to thoughts and feelings being dangerous in investigations? Didn't you tell me we're only interested in what we know and can prove?"

She pulled a face. "You're no fun! And anyway, this is speculation, which is totally okay if you ask me."

Still grinning, Fitzwilliam raised his mug of coffee to her. "Here's to a good healthy dose of speculation!"

The door opened, and Reed strolled in, followed by the lofty Prior, the lanky Turner, and a slim man in his mid-forties wearing a navy-blue suit. *I wonder who that is?* Fitzwilliam raised an eyebrow at Adler as they both rose and stood by their desks.

"We'll go into my office," Reed said as he walked across the room. Prior turned and nodded to Fitzwilliam and Adler as he followed Reed. Fitzwilliam suppressed a smile. *It looks like Reed is being chased by a giant.*

They followed the stranger into the cramped office. Prior and Turner filed in and made their way to the back of the space. *Sneaky! They've got the windows.* Leaving Fitzwilliam and Adler no choice but to fill the area in front of them.

"Fitzwilliam, Adler, this is Detective Chief Inspector Tim Street." Reed gestured towards the man with the short grey hair as they stopped in front of the desk. "DCI Street is from PaIRS but is currently on secondment to MI6."

Fitzwilliam caught Adler's eye. *MI6? Well, this has got interesting all of a sudden.* Although Fitzwilliam had never met DCI Tim Street before, he'd heard of the man. He'd briefly been his boss's boss before her promotion. 'Firm but fair' was how Copson had described him.

"Sir, this is DS Richard Fitzwilliam, who is temporarily on loan to us from Intelligence, and DS Emma Adler, who has been with my team for about six months now."

Street turned and held his hand out. "Adler, pleased to meet you. I hear good things about you from Reed here." Adler beamed. Reed, who was now standing to the chief inspector's right, cleared his throat and looked down at his shoes.

"And Fitzwilliam. You work for Frances Copson, I assume?" His handshake was firm and furious.

Fitzwilliam nodded. "Yes, sir."

"Then you're lucky to have such an inspirational boss. Learn all you can from her."

He's smooth... "Yes, sir, I will."

Street nodded in return, then crossed his arms and leaned back to rest on Reed's desk. "Without wishing to sound like a cliche, but what I'm about to tell you is top secret." He looked at the four faces in front of him, making sure he held each person's gaze for a few seconds, then he continued, "And by that, I mean only a handful of people know what I'm about to tell you. There's an excellent reason why, and I've no doubt it will become clear to you when I reveal why I'm here."

Do all MI6 people like to drag things on like this? Come on, pal, just tell us.

"James Wiltshire, the Earl of Rossex, had a special relationship with MI6."

What on earth does that mean?

"He was, shall we say, helping us to identify potential international threats."

The king's granddaughter's husband was working for MI6? Surely not...

"Do you mean he was working for MI6, sir?" Turner asked. He sounded as if he, too, was finding it hard to believe what they were hearing.

"Well, not exactly." Tim Street frowned. "The earl had his own responsibilities working for the royal family. But as part of the role, he had high-level contact with many leaders and senior movers and shakers from around the world. With the right training, the earl was able to make observations and report conversations to us that could be of importance to our national security."

He was a spy?

"He wasn't a spy, if that's what you're thinking." Street smiled, and Fitzwilliam felt a burst of heat rocket up his neck. "He was more of a keen observer who reported back to MI6 if he saw anything he felt would interest us. It was the earl who spotted the red flags in Riutia early last year that resulted in us foiling an attempted coup to overthrow the democratically elected leader there."

Wow! Fitzwilliam had been working in intelligence for much of his career, first at City and more recently within PaIRS, and he knew how strategically important the small island in the Indian Ocean was to the United Nations. He remembered when the rumours of trouble had first surfaced in intelligence circles and how concern for the stability of the region was high. Then suddenly, a few military leaders and presidential aids had been removed, and all had been right with the world again. *And it was the earl who triggered it all.* Fitzwilliam found a new respect for the dead man. *I'm sorry I never got to meet him.*

"It may surprise you to know there are several high-profile British citizens with an international reach who provide a similar service to their country."

Really? How did I not know that? But then, this was MI6, and they were known within the intelligence services as playing their cards very close to their chests.

"Anyway, back to James Wiltshire. The earl had an MI6 liaison officer who was his point of contact, and they spoke regularly. Four days ago the earl requested a meeting with his POC, and it was due to take place yesterday morning."

Ah, so that was the 'private errand' the earl had in London.

"I've spoken to the officer, and he reports the earl wouldn't say exactly what he wanted to see him about but told him it was something he'd been mulling over for a while. And that, I'm afraid, is as much as we know."

So why are you telling us this?

Street shrugged. "So you're probably wondering why I'm sharing this with you. I want you to bear it in mind when you're conducting this investigation. If you come across anything you think could be relevant, raise it to me please. I'm especially interested if anyone shares with you something that suggests what the earl wanted to talk to us about. It's just possible he said something to someone without them realising its relevance."

So was his relationship with MI6 relevant to his accident? *Is Street suggesting it wasn't an accident?* As he was about to open his mouth, Adler beat him to it.

"So are we now treating his death as suspicious, sir?"

Street unfolded his arms and stood up straight. "No, not at all. We still firmly believe the earl's death was a tragic accident. Nothing that has come to light so far has changed this view. However, we're keen to find out what the earl knew and was planning to talk to us about yesterday. And that's the only reason I have shared this with you today."

Prior cleared his throat. "Sir? Who else within the earl's close contacts and family knew of his special relationship with MI6?"

The chief inspector shook his head. "As far as we know, no one else knew. The reason it works so well is that these informants, for want of a better word, go under the radar. No one outside of MI6 and a few select members of the intelligence services know of their mission. In fact, I wouldn't be sharing this information with you if the earl was still alive. I cannot stress enough how vital it is this information doesn't go beyond those in this room. Do I make myself clear?"

They nodded.

"Good. Well, if there are no more questions, I need to get back to London. Here's my card" —he handing them each a business card— "if you need to contact me. Thank you for your time."

The lean man (*I bet he's a runner*) nodded at them all, then, patting Reed on the shoulder as he passed him, he left the room.

21

8:35 AM, THURSDAY 5 JANUARY

The Society Page online article:

__BREAKING NEWS Mystery Woman Was in the Earl of Rossex's Car__

The Daily Post *is reporting that an unidentified woman was also in the car that killed James Wiltshire (24), the Earl of Rossex, when it crashed in Fenshire late on Tuesday evening. The earl died at the scene, but it is rumoured the woman was alive when emergency responders arrived at the scene. She died from her injuries later in the hospital in the early hours of yesterday morning. The woman has not been named, and a police spokesperson was unavailable for comment at the time of going to press. However, sources at Francis Court, where the Earl and Countess of Rossex have a house on the estate, claim the dead woman was the wife of a member of staff.*

Meanwhile, at Francis Court, the Duke of Arnwall arrived home yesterday afternoon, having flown back from his Irish estate to comfort his daughter, Lady Beatrice (21), the Countess of Rossex. Lady Rossex's elder brother Lord Frederick Astley (24), Earl of Tilling, also arrived at Francis Court late last night, having been granted special leave from the Army to be with his family. The King and Queen, who are staying at nearby Fenn House, are said to be in close contact with their granddaughter and are expected to visit her in the next few days.

Flowers and tributes to James Wiltshire have been laid at the main gates to Francis Court, with many members of the public gathering to express their shock over the death of the grandson-in-law of the king. Barriers have been erected in the area, and the public are being asked to be patient if they wish to pay their respects. Other mourners have been visiting nearby Fenn House, as well as Gollingham Palace in Richmond, and London's

Knightsbridge Court, to lay flowers in remembrance of the late earl.

Books of condolence have been opened in various public buildings, including libraries, council offices, and many churches round the country.

22

8:45 AM, THURSDAY 5 JANUARY

Simon checked his watch again. *Why does time go so slowly when you're waiting?* He wondered how long the briefing Turner was in with Prior would last. Someone senior from PaIRS was here to talk to them apparently. He hoped they wouldn't be much longer. He was keen to get back to HQ and make himself useful, not sit around in a restaurant, as nice as it was, twiddling his thumbs. Glancing up, he caught the eye of the striking young blond man sitting with the woman wearing red glasses. The man smiled. There was something cheeky in his grin that made Simon smile back. *He seems fun.* Maybe a little loud and flamboyant. But very attractive…

Stop it! What would the lads at work think if they heard me? He looked away and picked up his coffee cup. *I should look at the woman he's with, not him!*

Simon sighed and put his cup down. Not for the first time, a feeling of guilt threatened to over-whelm him. *And what about Sharron?* His fiancée. So kind. So pretty. So loving. Sharron deserved his full attention. He needed to get a grip on his obses-sion with men and get back on track. *Settle down. Start a family. Do what is expected of me.*

He checked out the tall man in the jeans and waistcoat again, but he was huddled over the table with the blonde woman and didn't see him. *Just as well. Now get on with your job and leave the hand-some man to someone else!*

Simon pulled the report he'd brought to present to Turner and Prior towards him and flicked through the pages, summarising it in his head as he went. Neither the driver of the black Range Rover nor the black estate car had come forward. Even though Prior had told him PaIRS didn't want to put out an appeal so soon, Simon disagreed. If the other witnesses were correct, at least one, if not all, of the cars might have gone past the accident site before the emergency services had arrived. *They may have vital information.* He would raise the suggestion of an appeal again. He hated loose ends.

"So any questions?" Reed addressed Fitzwilliam and Adler as the three of them remained in his office.

I still can't believe it — James Wiltshire, the Earl of Rossex, a spy!

"I'm still gobsmacked, sir." Adler stood with one hand on her curvaceous hip, her head tilted to one side. "The Earl of Rossex was, to all intents, a spy." She shook her halo of dark hair, the tight curls springing backwards and forwards. "It's like a movie plot."

Reed, a smile tugging at his lips, said, "Just to be clear, Street told us the earl wasn't a spy."

That might not be what he called him, but when he described what the earl had used to do, it sounded like he'd been a spy to me.

"Yes, I know what he told us, sir." Adler grinned.

His brain making connections, Fitzwilliam considered the revelation about the earl and MI6. *Does it change anything?* Had someone tampered with the car before the emergency services had arrived? It was possible they'd opened the passenger door and the boot and had searched the vehicle. They might have even taken something from Gill's suitcase. *But what? And why?* Was he just being fanciful now? *Am I getting carried away just because of the earl's new status as an intelligence informant?* And what was it he had been chewing over for a while before deciding to tell his MI6 contact?

"Fitzwilliam?" Reed's voice cut through his thoughts.

"Sorry, sir. Yes?"

Reed folded his arms and leaned back on the front of his desk, mimicking Street's earlier stance. "I was just saying, let's not get carried away now we have this new information. It doesn't change the fact that the earl died in an unfortunate accident. All we can do is report back to Street if we find out anything pertinent to what the earl was going to raise with his contact. Okay?"

"But, sir." Fitzwilliam wasn't happy with the statement that it changed nothing. "Isn't there a possibility someone killed him to stop him talking?"

Reed uncrossed his arms and levered himself upright. "Why would you think that?" He leaned towards Fitzwilliam, the gaze from his green eyes fixed on Fitzwilliam's face.

Am I making an idiot of myself? Fitzwilliam was used to throwing out ideas within his intelligence team, however silly they might have appeared on the surface. Often, the wilder the theory, the more they'd discussed it, eventually toning it down to something that was possible, if not probable. However, it was becoming clear to him Intelligence was a unique environment, where instincts, theories, and thoughts were encouraged. In the investigations team, it was all facts and evidence. *Oh well, here goes...*

"Well, I think it's possible someone checked the car before the Maynards found it. There's a chance someone opened the passenger door and the boot and perhaps even searched Gill's case." Reed said nothing. Fitzwilliam swallowed. "And now we know the earl had some information for MI6. Isn't it possible it could have been about someone who was dangerous? I think we should consider this from the point of view that it could be murder." Still Reed said nothing. *Say something!*

Reed dropped his gaze and sighed. "Well, it's an interesting theory, Fitzwilliam. But unless you have evidence to support it, then I think it's unlikely to be the case. However, I will look over the statements you've taken from the Maynards, and I'll ask Forensics to determine from their examination of the earl's car if it's likely someone opened the door and boot post-crash. They will also, of course, test to see if anyone tampered with the car, but early indications suggest not. I'll ask them to give it a bit more consideration."

Fitzwilliam's eyes widened. *I wasn't expecting him to be so open to the idea.* About to turn to Adler and give her a smug smile, he paused as Reed continued, "But I have to say, I think you're getting a bit carried away. I don't know how someone would stage an accident like that and be sure the victim or victims died. So far, there's nothing to support the suggestion the crash was anything other than an accident. And why would they have searched Gill's belongings when it was James who was the MI6 informant? In the end, I will only consider facts and evidence. Is that understood?"

Is he just humouring me then?

Fitzwilliam nodded.

"Good. So"—he clapped his hands and rubbed his palms together—"I want you, Adler, to interview Alex Sterling, the husband of the woman who died. See if he knows why his wife was in the earl's car. Find out how well they knew each other. There is a DC from CID around somewhere. Take him with you, will you? He can take notes."

Adler nodded and headed for the door.

"You and I, Fitzwilliam, are off to interview the countess."

23

NOT LONG AFTER, THURSDAY 5 JANUARY

"So, DC Lattimore—"

"Simon, please."

Adler slowed down and smiled. "Er, Simon. Are you locally born and bred?"

"Yes, sarge. I was born just outside King's Town."

"So do you get to visit these large stately homes often?"

They made their way along the long drive — the original single-track road that led to the main house, Francis Court. The winter sun was still low in the sky, and its reflection bounced off the tarmac as it shone through the leaves of the trees lining the road. Adler pulled her sunglasses off the top of her head and dragged them onto the bridge of her nose.

Simon turned his head away from the sun's rays. *I shouldn't have left mine in the car.*

"Not really. I've only been in CID for a short while. Before that, I was in uniform and mainly worked in the town. I did a couple of escort duties when their majesties were being transferred from the station to Fenn House and a bit of crowd control when they did their walkabouts at Christmas and Easter, but that's all. This is my first time at Francis Court."

"It's an impressive estate," Adler said as they reached a track going off to their left. "We have nothing like this where I grew up in Brixton, that's for sure." She chuckled.

There doesn't seem to be any malice or envy in her comment, Simon thought. *She seems straightforward enough.* He wondered how hard she'd had to work to get into PaIRS. He was aware from a mate of his in the City Police how difficult it was to get selected to join those special project teams even when you were a man. *It must be so much harder when you're a woman.* His gaze suddenly caught a movement to his left, and he squinted into the forest of trees. *Deer!*

"Did you see that?" Adler asked, excitement in her voice as she moved closer to the woods and peered in.

"Yes. We get lots of them around here. This time of year, they travel in large groups."

"I've never seen one in real life before," she said, moving back to the path.

"Unfortunately, you're likely to see the smaller ones dead on the side of the road around here. They're so hard for driver to see, especially the young ones. They can do a fair amount of damage to your car as well."

Adler stopped to face him. "Do you think that's what happened to the earl? Did he hit a deer, do you think, and it sent him off the road, down the embankment, and into a tree?"

Simon shrugged as he, too, came to a standstill. "Quite a few of the witnesses who have come forward reported seeing a herd of deer around that night, so it's definitely a strong possibility."

She frowned. "You don't seem so sure, Simon. Is something bothering you about it all?"

She's perceptive too.

"It's nothing really, just a couple of witnesses that haven't come forward yet who I think might have seen something. I'd like to hear their stories before I put forward a theory of what happened."

"So you think it's suspicious these witnesses haven't come forward, do you?"

A little. It's not as if the case isn't getting loads

of publicity! In Simon's experience, a high-profile investigation like this brought out all sorts of people who wanted their moment of fame. *So why haven't the drivers of the two black cars come forward?* Unless, of course, they were up to no good. "I think it's odd with such a high-profile incident, the drivers and potential passengers of two vehicles haven't been in contact."

"But the witnesses also reported that the plates looked unusual or foreign, so maybe they're out of the country. Or they don't speak English. I can think of several reasons they've not come forward yet."

She's right. But even so...

He nodded.

She grinned. "I can see you're not convinced. You should talk to DS Fitzwilliam in my team. He's convinced someone opened the passenger door and the boot of the earl's car before the Maynards found them. Maybe it was your missing witnesses." She patted him on the arm and moved past him, heading towards a row of cottages over to their right.

Even though he knew she'd been teasing him, his heart quickened. *Could the two things be linked?*

24

MEANWHILE, THURSDAY 5 JANUARY

"Darling, are you sure you want to go ahead with this?" Her Royal Highness Princess Helen, daughter of the king and a well-respected senior member of the British royal family, paced backwards and forwards in front of a wall of floor-to-ceiling windows in the Green Sitting Room that looked out on the large expanse of lawn at the rear of Francis Court.

Bea sat on an adjacent two-seater sofa to where her mother was wearing a hole in the rug, fiddling with the rings on her left hand. Tension twisted the muscles in her neck, and she moved her head from side to side to relieve the stiffness. *I wish she'd stop pacing.* "Mother, please sit down. You're making me even more anxious."

Princess Helen stopped abruptly and moved to perch on the edge of the sofa opposite her daughter, on the other side of a low coffee table. "Sorry, darling, I'm just not sure this is such a good idea. It's too soon. You're still in shock." Placing her hands in her lap, she crossed her ankles and stared at Bea, concern etched on her face.

Bea gave her mother what she hoped was a reassuring smile, then looked away. *Is it too soon?* She didn't know. She knew nothing at the moment. Her brain was mush, and she was drained of all energy.

She'd spent the first sixteen hours since her mother had broken the news of James's accident observing the activity surrounding her as if she'd been watching a movie. Her mother, her sister, the staff — all fussing around her. A lot of handholding and awkward hugs. But it hadn't felt like it had been happening to *her*. James had died — shouldn't she have been crying, or screaming, or shouting? All she'd felt was sick. And that had been nothing new.

Even last night, curled up in bed with Penny snuggled up next to her, she'd just laid there. Her stomach had settled for the first time that day, listening to the dog's breathing. She'd tried to conjure up some emotion, but she'd felt nothing. *I'll wake up tomorrow, and it will all have been a bad dream.*

And when she'd woken up this morning, for a short while, everything had seemed so normal she'd almost believed her own lie. Then Mrs Fraser had appeared with coffee, and Lady Beatrice had known just by looking at the woman's red and puffy eyes that it was all very real. It hadn't just been a nightmare. James really *was* dead.

After the housekeeper had left, enveloped in wave after wave of nausea, the tears had finally come. Gut wrenching sobs had racked her already fragile body, and she'd prayed it would stop as she'd bitten down on her knuckles, trying to regain control of herself. She'd told herself she must remain strong. She was a member of the royal family. She was expected to be stoic in the face of disaster. *Dry your eyes, Bea. Crying won't bring him back.*

And so her thoughts had turned to the circumstances of James's death. *I need to know what happened.* Why had James been in the area on Tuesday night when he should have been in London? She'd spoken to him at around six that evening, and he'd not mentioned he was coming home. In fact, he'd told her he would ring her later before he went to bed. Her sister's theory was he'd been coming home to surprise her. *But why?* It was she who had news to share, not him, as far as she knew. And anyway, he had meetings in London planned the next morning. So why would he have driven all the way back to Francis Court if it meant he would have then had to turn around and go straight back to get there for first thing in the morning? It made no sense. *Why, James?*

"Darling?"

Her mother rose, but Bea waved her back down. "I'll be all right, Ma. I want to know what they've found out."

But that was only partly true. She dreaded finding out why Alex Sterling's wife had been in the car with her husband. As kind as everyone had been to her over the last twenty-four hours, even in her numb state, she'd noticed the change in how they'd treated her since the news had first broken that a woman had been in the car with James when they'd found him. Now the sympathy was mixed with pity. She'd seen it in their eyes. She knew what everyone was thinking. *Are they right?* She thought back to Sarah's comment a few weeks ago asking if James was having an affair. At the time it had seemed such a ridiculous idea, and they'd both dismissed it quickly. James wouldn't do that to her. He loved her. But now... Had they been wrong after all? Had James been having an affair with Gill right under her nose? A familiar wave of nausea washed over her, and she took a deep breath.

She needed answers. And the one person who could give them to her wasn't here anymore. Would never be here again…

Her head spun. She gripped the side of the sofa, willing the dizziness to pass quickly. *When will this all stop?* The sickness. The dizziness. The feeling of dread in the pit of her stomach. The sudden lack of breath. An empty hollow pit in her core had opened and was sucking up all of her energy. *Please make it stop.* She let go of the arm of the sofa and reached over to grab the glass of water from the coffee table. The cold liquid hit the back of her throat, and the need to run out of the room to the connecting cloakroom passed. She cleared her throat and took another sip of water before returning the glass to the table. *Come on, Bea. You can do this.*

25

ABOUT THE SAME TIME, THURSDAY 5 JANUARY

"Let me lead, Fitzwilliam," Reed whispered over the echo of their footsteps as they followed the formally dressed man in front of them across the black-and-white tiled floor. "It's going to be tricky, especially with Princess Helen there. We need to tread carefully."

Is he suggesting I won't know how to deal with them?

"It's not that I don't think you can handle it. But it's your first time meeting them in what I can only describe as difficult circumstances. They already know me, so it will be best if I am the one doing the talking. Okay?"

Fitzwilliam nodded. *So what am I supposed to do?*

"If you wouldn't mind taking a few notes for me. Just the essential facts. That would be very helpful. And then, once we're done, I'd value your opinion on what they said."

Fitzwilliam suppressed a sigh. *So, basically, keep quiet.* "Yes, sir."

They reached the bottom of the massive staircase that dominated the Painted Hall, its navy-blue carpet partly covering the stone stairs zig-zagging high above them to the first floor and beyond. The ornately carved gold-painted balustrade was topped with a thin smooth brass handrail. Fitzwilliam followed it up to the balcony visible on either side of the landing, where portraits (presumably of ancestors) hung and white marble busts sat on pedestals. Looking behind him, he saw the balconies met at a gold-and-red painted arch leading to a large wooden doorway.

"Impressive, isn't it?" Reed commented as Fitzwilliam whistled softly, his gaze drawn to the ceiling above them, which depicted the scene of a great Roman battle.

"And I thought Gollingham Palace was majestic."

Reed chuckled as they continued up the stairs. "Francis Court is actually older than GP. Henry VIII gave the land to the first Duke of Arnwall in the early fifteen hundreds as a wedding gift when he married Lady Charlotte Bridle, who was lady-in-waiting to his then-wife Katherine of Aragon."

"Now that beats a toaster!"

Reed laughed. "They completed the original house, church, and grounds in about twenty years, which in those days was quick. About two hundred years later, a fire destroyed a substantial portion of the house, and so they rebuilt it, this time in the Palladium style designed by architect Lord Burlingham. The ceilings here in the Painted Hall are a replica of the originals based on the paintings and drawings they had from that time."

"You should be a tour guide, sir," Fitzwilliam said as they reached the first floor and turned left.

Reed grinned. "I love the history of these old places. I feel very privileged to work in and around them."

Following the landing around to the right, the butler led them to a door halfway around the balcony, then pausing, he knocked.

"Here we go, Fitzwilliam," Reed said as the man opened the door and announced them.

"Detective Chief Inspector Angus Reed and Detective Sergeant Richard Fitzwilliam from PaIRS, ma'am."

26

10:02 AM, THURSDAY 5 JANUARY

Bea stiffened as the butler announced the two officers from PaIRS. *Here goes.* She rose at the same time as her mother but remained by the sofa, turning to inspect the two men. The older, shorter man she vaguely recognised looked quite relaxed as he entered the room, a smile splitting his face as he walked towards the princess.

"DCI Reed, it's been a while since you were last here." Princess Helen strolled across the room towards the door, holding out her right hand. Reed stopped and gave a short neck bow, then took the princess's hand and shook it.

Meanwhile, the younger man (*He must be the DS*) stood awkwardly by his boss's side, his arms behind his back.

"Your Royal Highness, this is Detective Sergeant Richard Fitzwilliam. He's new to my team, having moved over from Intelligence."

"Sergeant." The princess presented her hand, and Fitzwilliam shook it.

So no bow then. Bea bristled. Was this tall policeman one of those who didn't believe in tradition? Although it wasn't obligatory to bow or curtsy to a member of the royal family, she'd rarely come across someone who didn't follow the custom. Studying his rugged face from across the room, she guessed his age to be in his late twenties, maybe early thirties. The way he stood up stock straight (*He must be about six two, the same height as James)* with his hands balled by his sides led her to think he was ex-military. She caught his gaze, and for a moment, his brown eyes searched hers. *What is that look? Curiosity?* She looked away. Didn't he know it was rude to stare?

"Detective chief inspector, I believe you've met my daughter before?" Princess Helen walked towards Bea, followed by the two men.

Reed stopped before her and bowed before taking her hand. "I believe I met you and your husband a few months ago when you were at Gollingham Palace for a security briefing, my lady. May I offer you my most sincere condolences?"

Her eyes prickled as his gentle Scottish accent washed over her. Trying to get hold of her emotions, she breathed in deeply through her nose. *Come on, Bea, you can't crumble just because someone has a comforting accent.* She returned his handshake as she mumbled, "Thank you, chief inspector."

The man called Fitzwilliam reached around his boss and offered her his hand. "Likewise, my lady," he said, his brown eyes meeting hers as she placed her hand in his.

Likewise? She suppressed an unexpected desire to giggle. Tempted as she was to reply with, "Ditto," she simply nodded, quickly shook his hand, then turned back to the balding Reed standing before her.

"Shall we all sit down?" her mother suggested. Bea smothered a sigh. She wanted to get this interview over with as soon as possible, not make them comfortable as if they were here for a cosy chat. *I swear if she calls for tea...*

The two men took the sofa that had its back to the window, and the princess sat down opposite them. As Bea lowered herself onto the couch beside her mother, a wave of nausea washed over her. She grabbed the side of the sofa and held her breath until it passed.

"Are you all right, darling?" Princess Helen asked, her eyes full of concern as she poured a glass of water and handed it to her. Despite Sarah's pleading that she told their mother about her pregnancy, Bea had resisted the pressure. She needed time. Time to get her head around James's death. Time to come to terms with the fact she would now raise a child without a father. *Oh, James, how could you leave me to face this all on my own?*

She swallowed the bile rising in her throat as she nodded at her mother. "I'm fine," she said, her voice sounding shaky to her ears. She cleared her throat, took a sip of water, and gave the men sitting opposite a brief smile as she placed it on the table. "Shall we get on?"

"Maybe you could start by telling us how your investigation is going so far, chief inspector," the princess said.

As Reed brought her mother up to date with where the police were, Bea, only half listening, looked over the inspector's shoulder and gazed out the window in front of her.

Her eye caught a small tractor being driven by one of the gardeners. It pulled a trailer as it wound its way along the path running alongside the lawn, appearing to head towards a clearing just to the left. Business as usual. The thought stabbed her in the heart as if it was a knife. She resisted the pull to place her hand on her chest.

What will life look like for me now? What is going to be my *business as usual?*

Since their engagement eighteen months ago, her and James's lives had been inextricably entwined. There had been no her or him anymore, just them. The six months leading up to their wedding had been a maelstrom of activity. To prepare for their official foray into the world of working royals, she and James had travelled the length and breadth of the country, introducing the king's future grandson-in-law to the public. While in the background, the biggest wedding the country had seen for five years (her sister's two years before had been a quiet affair because of the recent death of the groom's father) was being planned by her mother, her grandmother the queen, and her future mother-in-law the Countess of Durrland, all with the help of various aids from Gollingham Palace. On the morning of their wedding day, the king had officially announced that he had bestowed the title of the Earl and Countess of Rossex on the happy couple as he'd welcomed them into the ranks of working members of the royal family, officially representing their king and country. Since then, they'd completed three tours abroad together, and apart from

James's trip to Miami in October and a few solo engagements, they'd rarely been apart.

So what happens to me now? Her stomach flipped at the thought of carrying out public engagements on her own. She had just about coped with the attention when she'd had James by her side. But on her own? And then, of course, there was the press. Her mother and sister had kept her away from the newspapers and television since James's death had been made public. But she knew they couldn't protect her for long against the comments and the speculation. And the questions...

"Beatrice?" Her mother nudged her. "Inspector Reed was asking if you have any questions?"

The two men sitting opposite her stared at her expectantly.

"Er, so have you found out why my husband was in the area last night when he was planning to be in London?"

They looked at each other, frowning, then the sergeant started, "We've already said—"

"No, my lady. I'm afraid not," Reed answered. "We understand he attended a meeting in London on behalf of your mother on Tuesday afternoon and was due to stay overnight at Knightsbridge Court prior to a private appointment on Wednesday morning."

Bea nodded, twisting the rings on her left hand. "Indeed."

He continued, "Apart from that, we know very little about his movements or what led him to return to Fenshire. I wonder if I can ask you a few questions about the last time you spoke to your husband, my lady?"

So they know nothing. She suppressed a disappointed sigh. "Yes, inspector. Go ahead."

"So when was the last time you talked to the earl?"

"Tuesday at about six in the evening."

"And did he say anything about his plans for the rest of the evening, my lady?"

"He told me he was going to order some food and get an early night."

"And how did he seem to you?" Fitzwilliam jumped in.

She frowned. He seemed a little overeager to have his voice heard. "Perfectly normal, sergeant."

"He wasn't upset or angry?"

Why is he asking? I've just said he sounded perfectly normal. She hadn't the energy for this. If they weren't able to tell her why her husband had been in the area, then...

Fitzwilliam cleared his throat. *How rude! I know you're waiting for me to answer your point-*

less question. Well, you can jolly well wait, Mr Impatient.

She leaned over the table in between them and picked up her glass of water again. She took a sip as she returned his gaze, then putting it down slowly, she said, "No, sergeant, because if he had, then I wouldn't have told you he sounded perfectly normal. Upset or angry was not how he normally was."

Next to her, her mother took a deep breath.

"Of course not, Lady Rossex," Reed immediately answered, pink spots appearing on his cheeks. He continued quickly, "We know he ordered food shortly after he spoke to you and it was delivered at seven, but the food remained untouched. Security checked him out when he left in his car just after seven-thirty. His overnight bag was still at the apartment when City Police searched it yesterday morning."

So he wasn't expecting to be away all night... Then Sarah's theory made little sense. If he'd been coming home, even as a surprise, surely he would've brought his bag back with him? *Oh, James, what made you leave so unexpectedly?*

"So do you have any idea why he would have left like that, without telling you or anyone else where he was going, my lady?"

She glared at Fitzwilliam. "What are you suggesting, sergeant?"

"I'm not suggesting anything, my lady. It just seems strange he would've left telling no one where he was going."

Unless he was up to no good. Is that what he's implying? Something bubbled up inside her. Her mind was in turmoil. Had James been going off to meet Gill? She knew she couldn't ignore the fact that they'd found the woman in his car with him. But why had he come all the way to Fenshire to see her when he would be coming back to Francis Court the next afternoon? It made no sense. She raised her hand to her forehead and slowly rubbed it with her fingertips. *What were you up to, James?*

She lifted her head and met the brown eyes of Fitzwilliam. "Indeed, sergeant, it seems unusual. So I hope you and the inspector here can find out why."

"Yes." Reed nodded enthusiastically. "Of course, my lady, that's what we'll endeavour to do."

"How was the earl in the weeks leading up to his accident, Lady Rossex?" Fitzwilliam asked.

What an odd question. Did the sergeant think James had had a premonition or something? *Shall I tell them that he was distracted and I thought something was worrying him?* She held the sergeant's gaze for a moment. *He'll probably think that supports his theory that James was having an affair. And, anyway, what difference does it make?* She suppressed a sigh. She didn't have the energy to do this. She broke contact with his eyes. "He was fine. Why do you ask?"

Fitzwilliam shrugged. "Just background."

Reed looked like he was about to ask a question, but Fitzwilliam continued, "According to his diary, my lady, the earl had private errands to attend to in London yesterday morning before he was due to return home here. Do you know what those were?"

What does it matter? He's dead! Her throat dry, she took another sip of water. "He was going to his tailors first thing, then meeting someone for brunch."

"Do you know who he was meeting and what they were going to be talking about?"

I don't know! Why all these questions? Why does it matter what he was planning to do the next day? She shook her head. "He didn't say, actually, but I think it was something to do with the Olympic bid."

"And how was your relationship with your husband, my lady? Were you on good terms?"

Good terms? What on earth does that *mean?*

Her energy levels were rising. This man was now seriously getting on what was left of her nerves. "My husband and I were on excellent terms, thank you, sergeant."

"And were you aware he was—" He hesitated as if struggling to find the right word. "*Friendly* with Mrs Sterling?"

How dare he! She jumped up. "I've just about had enough of your impertinence, sergeant."

Reed rose. "Lady Rossex, I'm so sorry. I can assure you—"

"I'm just trying to understand—" Fitzwilliam had also risen and was looking a little flustered.

She turned on him, her eyes blazing. "I don't believe you! Like everyone else, you think my husband was having an affair, and you want to know if I knew about it? Isn't that right, sergeant?"

He raised his chin and met her glare with a steely gaze. "Did you, my lady?"

"No!" she shouted, her eyes stinging now. "My husband wasn't having an—" She stopped, her throat constricting as she fought against the tears. She looked away and stumbled to the window, turning her back on the others. *Oh, James, why have you left me in this mess?*

"DCI Reed, I think that's enough for today, don't you?" Her mother's voice brokered no argument. Bea heard her walk towards the door and open it.

"Yes, of course, ma'am. I'm so sorry if—"

Reed was cut off by the princess. "No matter, chief inspector, you have a job to do, and we respect that. It's just my daughter is still in shock, and I fear she's overwrought. This was too soon for her. I think it's best you leave now, and we'll try again later. Harris!"

The butler appeared within seconds and ushered the detectives out.

A few minutes later, Bea felt an arm around her as the familiar smell of Yves Saint Laurent's Rive Gauche enveloped her. As she leaned into her mother's embrace, the tension left her, and the tears began to flow.

27

SHORTY AFTER, THURSDAY 5 JANUARY

"I'm sorry, sir." Fitzwilliam turned to Reed as they followed Harris down the carpeted stairs towards the Painted Hall below.

Reed nodded. "Let's talk about it outside, shall we?" His eyes moved towards the back of the man walking formally ahead of them.

Fitzwilliam suppressed a sigh. *Have I really messed it up so soon?* He'd no idea the seemingly disinterested Lady Rossex would turn on him like that. *Did I deserve it?* He pondered for a moment. On the one hand, he was just doing his job. She was a key witness, after all. She was the last person to have talked to the earl (presumably except for Gill Sterling) and the person who had known him best. They needed her to help them piece together the earl's last movements. On the other hand, she'd just lost her husband in what must be very trying circumstances for her.

They reached the bottom of the stairs, and Fitzwilliam was surprised when rather than turn right and walk them back to the north side door, where they had come in, the butler carried on straight ahead and led them across the black-and-white chequered stone floor. Fitzwilliam turned to Reed to question where they were going, but the inspector was looking around him, his mouth ajar. *Probably admiring the decor*, he thought. They continued to follow the straight back of Harris, and Fitzwilliam's mind returned to the encounter with Lady Rossex a few minutes ago.

Maybe he should have trodden a little more gently? But then, she'd seemed so aloof and un-emotional, he'd assumed, maybe incorrectly, theirs had been more a marriage of convenience than a love match. He knew from the background information he'd read last night that the countess and the earl had known each other since they had been young, their parents being good friends of the family. And it hadn't been a big surprise to anyone when they had announced their engagement eighteen months ago — it had been a suitable arrangement — the granddaughter of the king and the son and heir of the Earl and Countess of Durrland. He checked himself. They must have been great friends. It was understandable she'd been upset by his death. *But she was also so angry.* Had it been because of the other woman? He thought it highly unlikely the countess hadn't been aware of her husband's relationship with Gill Sterling, however much she'd protested. The aristocracy often had arrangements about that sort of thing, didn't they? As long as everyone was discreet about it. Was it the fact that it was now in the public domain that had made her furious? He imagined it must be very embarrassing when your husband was found dead in a car with his mistress…

"Thank you, gentlemen," Harris said as they reached what Fitzwilliam presumed to be the main entrance to Francis Court. The butler opened the large metal-studded wooden door. "Have a pleasant day." He bowed his head and stayed in the position as they walked past him and out into the bitter winter's morning. *Clank.* The door closed behind them as they descended the stone steps that deposited them in front of the famous fountain known as The Cascade. Fitzwilliam had previously only seen pictures of the towering water feature, with its twenty-two steps down which the water flowed rapidly.

"It's truly impressive, isn't it?" Reed commented as they came to a halt in front of the structure, his voice raised above the sound of the gushing water.

Fitzwilliam nodded.

"Right," Reed said, rubbing his hands together. "We need to get back to the office before we freeze to death." Pulling his sports jacket tight around his chest, he turned left and began walking along the path in front of the east wing of the house. Fitzwilliam shoved his hands in the front pockets of his navy-blue chinos and followed his boss.

"So, Fitzwilliam," Reed said as he got level with him. "I think that could have gone better, don't you?"

Sitting on the sofa facing the windows in the Green Sitting Room at Francis Court, Bea felt much calmer now. Had she really shouted at the impertinent sergeant from PaIRS? She could feel the heat in her cheeks. *How embarrassing!* But then she recalled his intrusive questions and bristled. How dare he talk to her like a common criminal!

She looked up at her mother, who was drinking a cup of tea opposite her. "Was I terribly rude, Ma?"

Princess Helen met her daughter's gaze. "Yes, darling. I'm afraid you were rather."

"But he was so—"

"Yes, I know, Bea. The sergeant's questions were rather direct. But they're just doing their job. They want to find out what happened to James as much as we do."

Bea slumped back into the sofa. The back of her eyes prickled. She raised her hand to her face and wiped under her eyes, which felt swollen and sore.

"Look, darling. I know you're trying to put on a brave face, and I really admire that. But we have to be so careful how we react with others outside of the family. You can't be publicly rude to people, Bea, however justified you feel." She sighed. "I can't imagine how hard this is for you, darling, and if you need to scream and shout, then you can do it with me and your father anytime you feel the need, but you must have more control around others. Do you understand?"

Lady Beatrice nodded as she leaned forward and picked up the black coffee in front of her. "Sorry, Ma," she mumbled.

"Darling, there's no need to apologise. You're in pain. Of course you are. I'm worried about you, Bea. Will you consider moving back here with us? I really think it would be for the best." Princess

Helen grabbed her daughter's hand and squeezed it. "I don't want you rattling around in that vast house on your own with just the Frasers and a handful of staff for company."

Bea sighed. Would it be best if she left The Dower House and moved back to Francis Court? It was very tempting. This had been her home for a lot longer than The Dower House had been, and if she was perfectly honest, it was James who had been keen for them to live independently as soon as they were married so they could establish their own household. She'd been perfectly happy sharing Francis Court and its staff with her parents, her paternal grandmother, and her older brother Fred when he was on leave from the Army. And now with a baby coming... She wasn't sure she could cope on her own. She put down her cup and dropped her mother's hand.

"What will happen to the Frasers if I come home?" She didn't want them to lose their jobs over this. They'd already lost so much.

"Well, here's what I'm thinking. Sarah could really do with some help. And although she's been resisting it until now, I think the reality of trying to keep on top of a large house with a young baby, a husband who is up in the city a lot, and with her due to come back to work soon..." Her mother took a sip of tea. "I think the Frasers could be a tremendous support to her and John."

Bea nodded. It would make sense. She looked out of the window at the empty green lawn in front of her (the grounds, normally open this time of year, had been closed for obvious reasons) and took a deep breath. Her life had been turned upside down — first finding out she was having a baby and then with James's death. *Everything has changed.* Life would never be the same. But at least if she was back at Francis Court, she would be somewhere familiar, protected, and around people she knew had her back. But first she would need to tell her mother about the baby…

"Ma, I have something I need to tell you…"

28

MEANWHILE, STILL MORNING, THURSDAY 5 JANUARY

"How did you get on?" Adler raised an eyebrow as Fitzwilliam and Reed entered the temporary offices attached to the Orangery in the grounds of Francis Court.

"I expect the order to have Fitzwilliam beheaded has just gone in," Reed replied as he walked past her and headed to his office. "Five minutes, please, and I'd like you both in my office for a debrief." He disappeared into his office and closed the door behind him.

"What happened?" Adler asked Fitzwilliam as she rose from her desk and headed over to the kitchen area to switch the kettle on.

Fitzwilliam threw himself into his chair and let

out a groan. "You know how I said I'm not very good with people?"

She poured water into two mugs and carried them back over. "Yeah," she said, placing a mug of steaming black coffee in front of Fitzwilliam.

He nodded at her to say thank you. "Well, it turns out I'm even worse with members of the royal family!"

A grin tugged at a corner of her mouth. "What did you do?" she asked, returning to her seat opposite him and placing her cup on the desk in front of her.

"I just asked the countess a couple of questions, and she blew up at me." Heat ran up his neck.

"What on earth did you ask her?"

"Just about her and her husband's relationship."

Adler took a sharp intake of breath. "Too soon!" she said, shaking her head.

He sighed. "She seemed so aloof and disinterested, I didn't realise she was upset…"

"Well, of course she's upset. Her husband's just died!"

"I know," he replied defensively. "But she really didn't seem like she was bothered, so I assumed it was a marriage of convenience and she knew about his relationship with Gill—"

Adler was grinning now. "Don't tell me you

asked her if she knew her husband was having an affair?"

He cleared his throat, the heat now in his cheeks. "I might have done," he mumbled.

She shook her head slowly, then took a sip of her tea. "Look, Fitzwilliam. Questioning someone in these sorts of circumstances is like when you're at the start of a new relationship. Take it easy, get to know them, let them come to trust you. You can't go in all guns blazing. You'll scare them off."

"Yes, well, as we know from the fact my wife is currently not speaking to me, I'm not good at relationships either," he said bitterly.

Adler jerked forward and spat out her tea. Laughing, she wiped her mouth. "Stop feeling sorry for yourself. You'll get the hang of it soon enough. Interviewing witnesses, I mean. I can't answer for your love life."

Reed's office door opened, and he called out, "Let's go."

She picked up her mug and waited for Fitzwilliam to do the same. As he got level with her, she smiled. "If it's any help, Lady Rossex has a reputation for being a bit difficult. Saunders had to deal with her a few months ago when there was some trouble at The Dower House. He said she really wasn't bothered and left it all to the earl to deal with. Between you and me, he said she was a bit stuck-up."

"That sounds about right," he said as they walked into Reed's office.

Adler took a seat in front of Reed's desk while Fitzwilliam perched on the back of the table opposite him.

Reed put down his pen and looked up at them both. "So let's talk about what new information we have. First, as you may have guessed, Adler, we didn't really get much out of the countess before the princess threw us out." He paused, then a grin appeared. "To be honest, as much as Fitzwilliam went in too bold and too soon, I don't think the countess knows anything more than us. She seemed genuinely surprised her husband had left Knightsbridge Court without eating the food he'd ordered, and I believe her when she said she didn't know where he was going." Reed nodded at Fitzwilliam. "I know you think she knew the earl was in a relationship with Gill Sterling, but I disagree. Her response, while maybe a bit of an overreaction to your question, sounded sincere to me."

Really? I think she's hiding something...

"Anything else you'd like to add, Fitzwilliam?"

Fitzwilliam pulled out his notebook and flipped

through the pages. He shook his head. "No thanks, sir."

"Adler, over to you."

Adler placed her mug down on Reed's desk and took out her pocketbook. "Well, sir, we have the earl's mobile phone records for the last month from Mr Glover. There was a call to the earl from an unidentified number a few minutes after seven on the evening of the accident. There are other calls in the period from the same number."

"And we can't trace it?" Fitzwilliam asked.

Adler shook her head. "We've tried ringing it, of course, but it appears to be dead. All we know is that it's a pay-as-you-go phone that was purchased using cash at a large supermarket in Clapham, London."

Could it be Gill's phone? But then why would it have been bought in London, not somewhere locally? *Anyway, don't we already know Gill's number?* "So it wasn't Gill's phone?"

"No. It's not her number."

What about the earl's MI6 contact?

"And it wasn't an MI6 number either. Street has already checked for us."

Whose is it then?

"Okay, thanks, Adler. I'm not sure it gets us

anywhere, but good work. How did you get on with Gill Sterling's husband?"

"According to Alex Sterling, he didn't know his wife and the earl knew each other socially. He couldn't account for why she was in the earl's car or why she had a bag with her but suggested she may have been going away for a few days to visit friends."

"Did she tell him she was planning to do that or leave a note to that effect?" Reed asked before taking a swig of his coffee.

"No, sir. Mr Sterling told us things had been strained between him and his wife for a while."

Fitzwilliam frowned. "Are there even any trains that run that late in this area?"

Adler shook her head. "According to Lattimore —he's the DC from CID who accompanied me to interview Mr Sterling— the last train from King's Town is ten forty-five in the evening, and the earliest is five forty-five the next morning."

"Didn't Mrs Sterling have a car of her own?" Reed asked.

"She did, sir, but it wasn't working. In fact, when Lattimore and I arrived at his cottage, Mr Sterling had his head in the bonnet of his wife's car. He said she'd told him it wouldn't start just before he'd gone on his business trip, but he'd not had a chance to look at it before he'd left."

That's odd... "So why was he trying to fix it now that she's dead?"

Adler shrugged. "People do strange things when they lose a partner. It's as if they haven't accepted the other person isn't coming back."

Reed nodded. "Well, if her car wasn't working, perhaps that explains why she ended up in the earl's. Did Mr Sterling have anything to say on the matter?"

"He speculated that maybe the earl was giving her a lift somewhere."

"When did Mr Sterling last see his wife?" Reed asked.

"The evening before, sir. He left early the next morning as he and a colleague were driving to Lincolnshire to see an irrigation system the estate is considering investing in. He says his wife was still asleep when he left."

Had he really not known about the earl and his wife? Fitzwilliam thought he could detect a note of something in Adler's voice.

She flipped over a page and continued, "They stopped off for dinner in King's Town and were driving back from there when he got the call from the police about the accident."

"And who was the colleague?" Fitzwilliam asked.

Adler slightly raised an eyebrow. "A Mrs Ellie Gunn. She's a part-time shift supervisor in the cafe here."

"What would a cafe supervisor be doing going to a meeting about irrigation systems?"

"He said she'd volunteered to go with him to take notes as she'd been a secretary in her previous role."

"Do you believe him?"

Adler shook her head. "No. The way he reacted made me think they're having an affair."

"Did you ask him?" Reed enquired.

"No, sir. It doesn't seem relevant to me. Mrs Gunn is off for a few days, but Lattimore is going to follow it up when she's back."

"Anything else?"

Adler shook her head as she returned her notebook to her trouser pocket.

"Okay, well, thank you both. I have a meeting with CID at their HQ now. Fitzwilliam, can you review the witness statements taken from the car drivers, and Adler, can you chase up the crime scene reports and the autopsies, please? I'll see you both this afternoon."

29

LATE-AFTERNOON, THURSDAY 5 JANUARY

"So, Adler, what have we got?" Reed asked as she and Fitzwilliam walked into his office that afternoon.

"Well, the preliminary reports are back, sir," Adler told him as she took a seat in front of his desk and opened her notebook. "The skid marks on the road and the trajectory of the car lead them to believe the earl was travelling between fifty-five and sixty miles per hour when he braked sharply and turned the steering wheel hard right. The wheels locked, and the car left the road, hitting the tree approximately twenty seconds later. The earl was killed on impact, as we know, and the passenger died later in the hospital. They haven't done the autopsy on Mrs Sterling yet. But they have completed the earl's, and he had no alcohol or drugs in his system."

"Thank you, Adler. Presumably they have concluded he swerved to avoid something in the road?"

"Yes, sir. The examination of the car doesn't suggest the earl hit anything other than the tree. There were no traces of car paint or animal flesh or fur anywhere on the car. They found fresh deer droppings in the middle of the road and by the hedgerows on both sides, but a search of the area found no wounded or dead animals."

"So possibly deer then?"

Or a car? Fitzwilliam cleared his throat.

Adler shrugged. "Possibly, sir. There were numerous sightings of deer in the area that night."

Reed tilted his head. "You don't seem convinced, Adler."

Adler glanced at Fitzwilliam. "It could have been a car he was trying to avoid, sir."

Reed looked from Adler to Fitzwilliam. "Do we have anything to support the theory it could have been a car?"

Fitzwilliam nodded. "Witnesses saw a black Range Rover in the area within the time frame of the accident, sir. It was seen at eleven-ten at one end of the road the earl came off, and again, along with another vehicle, a black estate, at eleven-twenty at the other end of the road, sir. With the time of accident being from eleven to eleven-thirty, it's likely at least one, if not both vehicles would have driven past the scene or—"

"Caused the accident?" Reed finished for him. "And these are the vehicles with the drivers who haven't come forward yet?"

"Yes, sir."

Reed pushed his chair back away from his desk and raised his hands to his chin, resting his face on them. He closed his eyes.

What's going on? Fitzwilliam glanced at Adler. She gave him a wry smile.

Reed's eyes pinged open. "How reliable are these witnesses, Fitzwilliam?"

"I've spoken to them myself this afternoon, sir. Both confirm they saw a black Range Rover, but neither could be more specific in terms of model or recall any of either of the number plates. The wife of one witness, who saw them with their hazard lights on, said she assumed it was royal security or police protection. She seemed to think she'd seen similar vehicles in the area before. But I've checked, and neither PaIRS nor Fenshire CID had vehicles in the area at the time of the accident. She also said she thought the number plate wasn't a UK one but when pressed just said it was a different shape. The other witness, who saw the Range Rover and the estate car later, didn't get a better look as both vehicles were travelling at speed."

"Then how can he be sure it was a Range Rover?" Reed asked.

"He recognised the vehicle's profile as he has one himself. His is white though."

Reed nodded. "And number plates. Did he get a look"

Fitzwilliam grimaced. "He also said he thought it looked different but wasn't able to expand any further."

Reed shook his head. "What about the occupants of the missing vehicles?"

"Again, the second witness wasn't much help there and couldn't confirm how many passengers were in each vehicle. The first couple had a much better look at the Range Rover and report two well-built men in the front, one on his phone. The female witness said they looked like security types, sir."

"What does that mean?" Adler asked.

Fitzwilliam shrugged. "She couldn't expand on her comment. She just said that she got that impression."

"Umm." Reed stroked his greying beard. "Okay, well, I think it's worth checking with other forces to see if they had anyone in the area."

"Yes, sir, I'll get on that. I've also spoken to my contacts back in Intelligence, and they're looking to see if any vehicles matching those descriptions show up on any CCTV cameras anywhere near here that night."

Reed nodded. "It's worth a try, I guess." He sighed and rubbed his beard. "But if we get no more solid information about these vehicles within the next hour, then we'll put out an appeal for the witnesses to come forward. Anything else?"

Fitzwilliam turned to Adler. "Did the report on the earl's car suggest someone had opened any of the doors or the boot of the earl's car post-impact?"

She shook her head. "I called and ask the question. They said there was too much damage to the car, so it's impossible to tell."

"And Gill Sterling's bag that was slightly open?"

"No fingerprints other than Mrs Sterling's. They did comment it looked like she'd packed the bag in a hurry as she hadn't folded the items on the top. She'd just stuffed them in."

Fitzwilliam frowned. *In a hurry, or did someone go through the bag, looking for something?*

"What about footprints at the scene? Anything interesting there?" Reed asked.

Adler frowned and flipped through her notes.

"Er, hold on. I have that somewhere. Here we go. Ah, yes. Because of the volume of emergency services personnel on-site, they weren't able to identify all the footprints individually. But they did group them together. You know: fireman's boots, police issue boots, etc. The only ones that didn't fall into one of those groups were Mr and Mrs Maynards, and two sets of, for want of a better description, 'others'."

That sounded promising. Could they belong to the person or persons who had opened the passenger door and the boot?

"Before you get too excited, Fitzwilliam. The scene of crime officer stresses these could also belong to emergency workers who were not wearing regulation boots."

Okay, I suppose that's possible, but it's worth investigating... "Did they give any more details about the 'other' footprints?" he asked eagerly.

Adler closed her notebook. "Not much, but it's in the report. I'll forward it to you."

"Thanks."

Reed nodded. "Okay, well we still have some work to do, but on the whole, I'm still inclined to believe the most likely scenario is that the earl, who was driving close to the legal speed limit, swerved to avoid a deer or maybe more than one, and subsequently came off the road and crashed."

But why is that more likely than the car? Fitzwilliam cleared his throat.

Reed raised his hand. "I'm not totally ruling out at this stage your theory another vehicle could have been a catalyst. However, we must be very careful about putting forward hunches or guesses." He lowered his hand and sighed, meeting Fitzwilliam's gaze. "It's possible we'll never know for sure exactly what happened, and unless we know for sure, then we have a responsibility not to present anything to the family or the public we cannot support with facts or evidence. Okay?"

Fitzwilliam nodded.

Reed looked at his watch. "All right, well, I have to be in London this evening, so I need to dash. Let me know if anything new comes up, and I'll see you both tomorrow afternoon."

30

EARLY EVENING, THURSDAY 5 JANUARY

The Society Page online article:

Earl of Rossex Conspiracy Theorists Get Busy as Police Appeal for Witnesses to Come Forward

Conspiracy theorists have had an online posting frenzy over the last few hours after Fenshire CID released a statement appealing for the occupants of two vehicles to come forward following the death of James Wiltshire, the Earl of Rossex, in a car crash late on Tuesday evening.

The appeal specifically asked for the drivers and passengers of a black Range Rover and a black estate car who witnesses saw in the vicinity of the accident to contact them immediately. This request has prompted speculation in the popular press that the accident may have involved more than just the earl's car. However, conspiracy theorists have taken it to another level and have been posting in chatrooms and forums their thoughts that the earl was deliberately run off the road by anti-royalists. One anonymous online contributor on the forum CT-Truth wrote, "The earl was a much admired member of the royal family and he and his wife were spearheading a resurgence in the monarchy's popularity. The anti-royalists have responded by putting out a hit on the earl."

A spokesperson for Fenshire CID stated, "Unfounded speculation is unhelpful to our investigation and upsetting for the earl's family. The two vehicles that were seen in the area may have witnessed something that will aid us in completing a picture of what happened to the earl two nights ago." When pushed by a reporter from The Daily Post, *the spokesperson confirmed that their current theory is that the earl swerved to avoid a herd of deer. He reiterated they do not believe a third party was involved.*

An article in The London Recorder *begged the question why conspiracy theories are so popular when someone world-famous dies. Professor Alan Mendham, head of Journalistic Studies at Exeter*

University, explained, "Sometimes an event can be so cataclysmic for society that a mundane explanation feels inadequate. In those circumstances, conspiracy theories offer a solution that is proportional to how enormous the event itself feels."

Meanwhile, tributes to the earl continue to stack up at the main gates of royal palaces around the country and Francis Court in Fenshire, with mourners still flooding to the venues to pay their respects to the popular royal. There have also been queues at some local libraries and council offices as the public wait to sign the local books of condolence that were opened first thing this morning.

31

LATE EVENING, THURSDAY 5 JANUARY

"Amber, at last!" On the fifth ring and just as he was about to give up, Fitzwilliam's wife picked up the call. He perched on the end of his hotel bed and crossed his legs.

"What does that mean?" she barked back. "I texted you three hours ago to say I was free to talk, and I heard nothing back."

Fitzwilliam suppressed a sigh. *She's still mad at me.* He wanted to move on, but it seemed she wasn't ready to let it go just yet.

"Sorry, love. All I meant was it seems like ages since we actually spoke. You know I'd rather talk than text."

"Yes, well, *you* know the reception at my parent's house isn't great. Text is more reliable."

Really? That's the first he'd heard about it. He suppressed a sigh. It wasn't worth arguing about. "Okay, I'll remember that. So are you going to the cottage in the morning?" He hoped she could still make the most of the break even though he wouldn't be there with her. Maybe the calming sea would have a positive effect on her and make her see reason…

"Does that mean you definitely won't be able to make it then?"

His heart sank. He could hear the pain in her voice.

"I'm sorry, bird. I'm going to be stuck here for a while longer. There really is a lot to do."

There was silence at the other end. He didn't want to fight anymore. Maybe he could make her laugh. "You'll never guess what happened today when I went with Reed to interview Lady Rossex. I—"

"I'm not interested, Rich. I don't care if you interviewed the king himself. What I care about is us. But it seems I'm the only one who does!"

He sprung up off the bed. *How can she say that?* Everything he was doing was for them. For their future.

"That's not fair, Amber. I had to come—"

"No, you didn't!" Her voice was shriller. "You

didn't need to take this assignment. Knowing how I felt, you could've turned it down. Then I would know we are more important to you than your career. But you didn't…"

He paced up and down by the side of the bed. How could she expect him to turn down a golden opportunity just to have a few days away by the sea? They could do that any time…

"But I'm doing this for—"

Click. The line went dead. Fitzwilliam stopped pacing and threw his mobile on the bed. *What on earth is wrong with her?*

Dave: *Do you want to go out for a drink tonight? x*

Amber: *Yes, please! What are your plans for the next few days? x*

Dave: *I don't really have any. Why? x*

Amber: *Do you fancy a few days away in a cottage by the sea? x*

32

MID-MORNING, FRIDAY 6 JANUARY

The Society Page online article:

Late Earl's Passenger Named as Gill Sterling

The police have this morning confirmed the woman who died alongside James Wiltshire (24), the Earl of Rossex, was Gill Sterling (27), the wife of Francis Court's estate manager Alex Sterling (30).

Ever since Mrs Sterling was unofficially named by a local newspaper, The King's Town Crier, *yesterday afternoon, there has been much speculation in the popular press about why Mrs Sterling was in the earl's car on Tuesday evening. In an interview with* The Daily Post, *Mrs Sterling's husband Alex suggested his wife may have been off to visit friends in Scotland while he was away on business, and the earl had offered her a lift to a nearby train station as her car was out of service. When asked if rumours of an affair between his wife and the earl were true, Mr Sterling categorically denied there was any relationship between them.*

A spokesperson for the Countess of Rossex refused to comment on the speculation, stating, "We would like to ask the public and the press to be mindful that the Countess of Rossex has lost a beloved husband and the Earl and Countess of Durrland have lost their much loved only son and heir. Please respect their privacy at this time."

Earlier this morning, Their Majesties the King and Queen greeted the crowds as they viewed the floral tributes left at the gates of Fenn House and read some cards and messages left for the earl by well-wishers.

At Francis Court, Her Royal Highness Princess Helen, along with her husband Charles, the Duke of Arnwall, their son Lord Frederick Astley, their eldest daughter Lady Sarah Rosdale, and Lady Sarah's husband John Rosdale also met the public this morning when they visited the main gates to see the tributes left for the Earl of Rossex. Lord Fred and Lady Sarah did a brief walkabout and thanked the crowds for coming out on such a wintry day. Lady Sarah told a member of the public that her sister Lady Beatrice was 'bearing up' and was touched by the warmth of everyone's support. Before they headed back inside Francis Court, the Astley family waved to the crowd, who in turn cheered.

33

LATE-MORNING, FRIDAY 6 JANUARY

"So as Reed is not due back until later this afternoon, I need you to come with me, Fitzwilliam." Prior leaned on the wall in the temporary PaIRS office at Francis Court, his arms folded.

Fitzwilliam suppressed a groan. Since first thing this morning, when the Astley family had requested an update, he'd been hoping to avoid having to attend the briefing. The last thing he wanted to do was see the young widow and her family again. In fact, he couldn't believe Reed had sanctioned it after what had happened last time.

"And before you ask, it was Reed's idea I take you. He said something about redemption."

Fitzwilliam gave a wry smile while Prior continued, "The countess will be accompanied by her elder brother Lord Frederick Astley. I've met him a few times before. He's an intelligence officer in the army, and he should be a calming influence."

"And what will you tell them, sir?"

"That the evidence suggests it was an accident probably caused by deer in the road, and we don't know why Mrs Sterling was in the car with the earl. There isn't really much else to say."

Fitzwilliam nodded. "And what about the Range Rover and the black estate car seen in the vicinity at around the time of the accident? Is there any news on them after the appeal?"

Prior sighed. "No. Which is all very embarrassing as it's stirred up so much more speculation in the press and online than we'd imagined. It would be so much easier if we had a result from the appeal to shed some light on what happened that we could share with the countess and her brother. But we don't right now, and that leaves us in the same position as before. We have some unidentified vehicles seen in the area, possibly around the time of the accident, whose occupants haven't come forward yet. What help is that to them or indeed anyone? It's my plan to say nothing about it. I only want to talk to them about what we actually know at this time."

Fitzwilliam sighed and nodded slowly. When

Prior put it like that, it sounded too vague. But he still had such a strong feeling it *was* relevant. Maybe it was best they said nothing. "Yes, sir."

"Good. So I'm happy to lead, but if you need to ask anything on behalf of PaIRS, then give me the nod and go ahead."

Fitzwilliam nodded. *I'd best stay quiet…*

"Right. Well, I have a few calls to make. We're due up at the house at two, so I'll swing by at one-thirty so we can walk up in plenty of time. Okay?"

"Yes, sir."

"I still don't understand why Reed wants me to go. I imagine I'm the last person Lady Rossex will want to see," Fitzwilliam said to Adler as he un-wrapped a chicken and bacon sandwich and threw the packaging into the bin between their desks in the PaIRS office. "Why can't you go? You're more senior than me in this team anyway."

Adler raised a dark eyebrow. "Have you finished whinging now?"

He let out a deep sigh. "Yes, I suppose so." He took a large bite of his lunch.

She smiled. "Look, I know you're embarrassed about seeing her again. I get that, but—"

"Hold on," he said through a mouthful of food. "I may have gone in a little strong in the circumstances, but it was her who massively overreacted. I'm not embarrassed. I just don't know if I can do subtle."

Adler laughed as she picked up a bottle of fruit juice and unscrewed the top. "I'd say that's a no!"

"Well, can you help me?"

She took a gulp of her drink, then said, "I think your best strategy will be to say nothing. Let Prior do the talking, and unless the conversation naturally goes down a route that allows you to ask something without it appearing forced or out of context, then just listen. What do you want to ask anyway?"

"I think we should try to find out more about the earl's relationship with Gill Sterling. They must have known about it, surely?" He placed the remains of his sandwich on the table and picked up his coffee.

"Why?" Adler asked, shaking her head. "Why is his relationship with Gill relevant to the accident?"

"Well, how do we know if it is or isn't if we can't get any answers to what was going on between the two of them?"

She tilted her head to one side. "I still don't get it. Whatever their relationship was, I don't see how it changes the fact that the earl swerved to avoid something and came off the road. Done. If they were having an affair or not, it doesn't matter." She dropped her empty juice bottle in the bin and continued, "I understand your interest in the black Range Rover. It's possible *it* caused the accident, not a herd of deer, and I don't like the thought someone is out there right now, not being held accountable for their involvement in the earl's death. But this, Fitzwilliam? I don't see what difference it makes."

Was she right? Did it really matter? He took another sip of his coffee and placed the mug down. *It's just...* "I don't like loose ends, that's all. Plus, I think the countess and her family know more than they're letting on and that bugs me."

She sighed. "You're going to have to stop letting how you feel get in the way. Investigation is about facts and evidence. Sure, you use your experience to guide you on how best to get to those facts and that evidence. Sometimes, maybe even a bit of intuition will tell you something isn't right and you need to look into it deeper. But you need to accept there will be loose ends. People will keep things from you. And you have to know when it matters and when it..." She trailed off, then gave him a shy smile. "Sorry, I'm not trying to tell you how to do your job. I just think this is different to what you were doing before, and…" She shrugged.

She's right. Fitzwilliam smiled at her reassuringly. "Don't worry. I value your opinion, and you're right. This is all new to me. I have to approach it differently. I can see that. So I will listen and learn and try not to open my mouth." He rose, and picking up his pocketbook from the desk in front of him, he slid it into the back pocket of his trousers. Grabbing his coat from the back of his chair, he grinned. "Wish me luck."

Adler grinned back. "Good luck, and try not to get thrown out a second time."

Adler: *Some info about the vehicles has come in. Let me know when you're done.*

Fitzwilliam: *On my way back now.*

Adler: *How did it go?*

Fitzwilliam: *We got thrown out again!*

. . .

Adler: *You're joking right?*

Fitzwilliam: *I wish I was.*

Adler: *What happened?*

Fitzwilliam: *Will tell you all about it when I get back. ETA 5 mins.*

34

MID-AFTERNOON, SATURDAY 7 JANUARY

Fitzwilliam strode along the side of the Orangery, the mid-afternoon sun bouncing off the glass structure and creating shimmering lights on the path in front of him. *I can't believe I did it again!* He let out a deep sigh. *I'm not sure I'm cut out for the investigative side of PaIRS.* Intelligence was his comfort zone. *Maybe I should stick to what I know.*

"It wasn't that bad, Fitzwilliam," Prior walking beside him said. "It's always tricky dealing with the bereaved. They get very defensive on behalf of their loved one. And in this case, the press speculation about the earl and Mrs Sterling has reached fever pitch. That can't be helping Lady Rossex much."

That was clear by the way she'd rounded on

him again. But then he'd promised himself he'd just listen and not say anything, so why had he felt the need to ask again about the relationship between the earl and Mrs Sterling? "I shouldn't have asked, sir."

They reached the temporary offices, and Prior stopped in front of the door to the one allocated to CID. "It wasn't an unreasonable question, Fitzwilliam, and it was Lord Frederick who raised it. Anyway, it's our job to understand what happened." He smiled and shook his head. "However, it's clear from what his lordship said that they expect us to finish this up quickly so they can arrange the funeral and then the family can move on. I fear we'll never know why the earl was in Fenshire that night or why Mrs Sterling was in his car. But as long as we're comfortable we've done as much as we can reasonably do, then we can do no more. I'll catch up with Reed when he arrives and get his view."

"Yes, sir."

Prior turned and entered his office while Fitzwilliam carried on to the office two doors down.

As soon as he walked in, Adler handed him a mug of steaming black coffee. "I thought you might need this," she said as she returned to her desk and picked up a mug of tea.

"Thanks," he said, putting it down on the desk in front of him and removing his coat.

"Well?" she asked eagerly, taking a sip of tea.

He sighed and sat down opposite her. Grabbing his cup, he took a sip of the hot liquid and leaned back in his chair. Stretching his long legs in front of him, he told her about his second disastrous encounter with Lady Rossex.

It had all gone well initially. The countess had seemed more engaged than at their first meeting, although he'd thought she seemed jittery from the start. Lord Frederick had asked pertinent questions to fully understand what they knew. Prior had told the Astley siblings about the theory of the deer, and his lordship had asked about the results of the accident scene reports and the autopsy. He'd seemed relieve to find out the earl hadn't been drinking and his speed had been within reasonable range of the limit on that type of road.

As Fitzwilliam recalled what had happened to Adler, it still surprised him at how quickly it had changed direction. "And that's when it all went wrong."

Adler tilted her head to one side, her brown eyes shining.

He continued, "First, Lady Rossex asked if the drivers had come forward following the appeal.

Prior told her not yet, but that it was still early days. I could see she wasn't at all happy about it. She said that she hoped it wasn't going to be a dead end after all the trouble it has caused."

Adler raised an eyebrow. "Does she mean all the press speculation, do you think?"

Fitzwilliam nodded. "Then Lord Frederick asked if we'd found out anything about Mrs Sterling's movements on that night and how she'd ended up in the earl's car. I could see Lady Rossex was getting agitated, and that should have put a warning shot across my bow. Anyway, Prior said we'd not been able to find out much so far, and Mr Sterling had been little help either. His lordship then asked Prior what Alex Sterling had said about the relationship between his wife and the earl. And I have to say, I read it as him trying to find out how much we knew." He picked up his coffee and took a gulp. He still thought that was what had been going on, despite what had happened next.

"And?" Adler leaned over her desk, her hands gripping her mug of tea.

"So I asked him if there *was* a relationship between Mrs Sterling and the earl. And the next thing I know, Lady Rossex jumps up, shouting she already told me once there was no relationship between her husband and the woman. She then accused me of being as bad as the press with my insinuations and stormed off to the other side of the room."

Adler shook her head. "Oh no," she mumbled.

"And do you know what hacks me off the most? I wasn't even asking her! But before I could defend myself, her brother rushed over to comfort her. After a mumbled conversation between them that I couldn't hear properly, he came back to us, thanked us for our time, and said he thought it was best we leave now."

"Wow, that's a proper dismissal."

Fitzwilliam blushed. "He's quite a straight-talking man, as you would expect with his military background." He hesitated and gave a wry smile. "I actually like him."

"So you left?"

Fitzwilliam nodded. "Pretty much. There was one other thing. As we were leaving, he said to Prior that he was sure we understood the importance of getting the inquiry wrapped up as soon as possible so the body could be released and the funeral arranged. He said any further delay would cause additional upset for the royal family and give the press even more opportunity to speculate."

"And what did Prior say?"

"Something very diplomatic, like, yes, we understand the stress this investigation is causing the countess and her family, and both CID and PaIRS were making it a priority to close the inquiry as soon as possible."

"Good response."

"When I left Prior just now, he said he would talk to Reed when he got back." He frowned. "Surely we can't be finished already? There's still the Range Rover and the estate car to trace, and we've done nothing but basic background checks on the earl or Mrs Sterling as far as I know, and—"

Adler put her hand up. "I have some news on the vehicles."

Really? Fitzwilliam's heartbeat rose. *Have the drivers come forward? Did they see what happened? Have they confessed to causing the accident?* His eyes widened, and he sat upright.

"Reed rang in to say he was leaving London to come back here while you were with Prior and the Astleys. He'd just had a debriefing with Street. You know the guy who was here and told us about the earl's involvement with MI6?"

Fitzwilliam nodded. *Where is this going?*

"Anyway, Street told him he's been contacted by a senior foreign diplomat whose four-man security detail, who were in a black Range Rover and a black estate car, got lost locally on Tuesday evening at the same time as our witnesses reported seeing the vehicles. His presence in the county was all hush-hush apparently."

"So did they see anything?"

Adler shook her head. "Apparently not."

Fitzwilliam's shoulders sagged. So the witness had been right. It had been security personnel she'd seen. But how could they have seen nothing when witnesses placed them in the area between eleven-ten and eleven-twenty? Unless the witnesses' timings were way out. Or the accident had occurred nearer eleven-thirty — the upper limit of the estimated time of death. He'd have to look at the security driver's statements and see exactly what time *they* had said they had been in the area...

"I think that closes down that loose end, don't you?" Adler stood up and moved to the kettle, tapping the switch to turn it on.

He drained the last dregs of his coffee and sighed. "Yes, I suppose so." He'd ask Reed for more details when he got back, but that seemed to be that as far as he could see.

"So I hear you really are off to the Tower of London this time, Fitzwilliam!" Reed said as he entered the room two hours later and headed towards his office.

Adler put her hand over her mouth to cover the grin on her face.

Fitzwilliam jumped up. "It would appear so, sir."

"Well, let's see if we can get this wrapped up before they come to take you away. My office, five minutes, both of you," he said, nodding to the two sergeants as he sailed into his office and closed the door.

"Do you think I'm in trouble?" Fitzwilliam asked the smirking Adler.

She shrugged. "I hear it's not as bad in the Tower as it used to be, and it's very conveniently located in the centre of the city."

"Helpful," he muttered as he plonked himself back down in his chair.

Adler cleared her throat.

What?

She had her elbows on the desk, her hands raised like she was about to give him a blessing.

"What?"

"Er, your turn to make the tea. I'll have a camomile one, please. Maybe you should have one too. It has calming properties, you know."

"Funny," he said sarcastically as he got up and

moved over to the kettle. Filling it up, he switched it on, and while it boiled, he rinsed two mugs in the sink before placing them out in front of the kettle. He dropped a camomile tea bag into the mug with a picture of Lionel Richie and the words 'Hello. Is it tea you're looking for?' printed on the front. The outside door opened, and Prior walked in.

"Ah, tea. Just what I need. White, one sugar, please, Fitzwilliam." He walked across the room to Reed's office door just as it opened.

Reed poked his head around the door and caught Fitzwilliam's eye. "Ah, perfect timing. Coffee, please, Fitzwilliam. White, no sugar." He grinned as he ducked inside, followed by Prior.

Great! Fitzwilliam turned to the sink and washed two more cups.

"So as far as everyone up at PaIRS HQ is concerned, we're ready to close the investigation and prepare our report for the inquest. Matt, how are CID about that?" Reed turned to his colleague while he picked up his mug of coffee with 'I don't need Google. My sergeant knows everything' emblazoned on the front.

Prior put down his mug of tea, which read

'There's a chance this is beer' and nodded. "We're good with that."

Fitzwilliam suppressed a huff. *How can you both be happy with closing the investigation now? There is so much still to look into...*

"Fitzwilliam, you look like you want to say something," Reed said, putting down his coffee.

Should I tell them what I think? Or would it be best to just keep his mouth shut? These were experienced senior police officers. *They must know what they're doing...*

"Erm, it's just, I've not been involved in an investigation like this before, sir." He'd not been involved in any PaIRS investigation before, but he wasn't going to share that right now. "But I'm surprised we're closing it down before doing more background checks on the victims, especially Mrs Sterling and—" He stopped when Reed held up his hand.

"There's been no crime committed, Fitzwilliam. That's the determining factor here. I know you had your concerns about the two vehicles seen in the vicinity of the accident site, but that's been cleared up now, and there are no other loose ends as far as I can see. We have the autopsy reports, the scene of crime report, and the witness statements. Nothing in them suggests this was anything other than an accident. So we don't need to do any more digging. It won't impact the outcome, and therefore it's unnecessary."

He shrugged. "Would it be satisfying to understand why the earl came back to Fenshire on the night of the accident when he should've been in London? Yes. Would we like to explain why Mrs Sterling was in the car with James Wiltshire when it hit the tree? Yes, of course. But knowing either or both details won't change the fact that the earl was travelling at a fairly brisk speed, swerved to avoid something in the road, and lost control of his car."

He crossed his arms and held Fitzwilliam's eye. "Okay?"

Was it okay? It didn't feel to Fitzwilliam like they'd done a very thorough job, but clearly both Reed and Prior felt they had done enough for them to close the investigation. Or was it just that they were under pressure to get the inquiry closed as soon as possible? Especially after the appeal, which had caused even more speculation and had clearly upset the Astleys, had led them to a dead end.

"Fitzwilliam?" Reed prompted.

"Sorry. Yes, sir."

"Great, well, Prior and I will start compiling our inquiry summary. Can I ask you both to go back now and drop all your supporting documents and any reports you have on a memory stick and let me have them before I leave? Thanks."

Adler and Fitzwilliam nodded and, rising, left the office.

He walked to the sink, dropped the mug he'd been using with 'Surely not everyone was Kung Foo fighting?' on its side (which he presumed belonged to the officer currently up a mountain) into the bowl, and exhaled loudly. There was an uneasy feeling in his stomach. *This doesn't feel right to me...*

35

FIRST THING, SUNDAY 8 JANUARY

"How did you get on last night?" Adler asked Fitzwilliam as he walked into their office. She handed him a mug of steaming black coffee.

"Thanks," he said as he took the drink, then he set it down on his desk and took off his coat. "She didn't get back to me. I think she must have poor signal." He sat down and grabbed his coffee.

Adler, now sitting back down in her chair at the desk opposite him, frowned. "What?"

"My wife. She's not answering my calls. But I'm hoping it's just because she has poor phone signal where she's staying."

Adler's face cleared. "Oh, your wife…"

Fitzwilliam was confused. *But she just asked how I'd got on… Oh…* "You meant about jotting down my concerns about the case, didn't you?" Yesterday evening Adler had suggested he did the exercise to help him get his thoughts straight before their meeting with Reed and Prior this morning. A slight pink tinge coloured his cheeks.

"Yes." A huge grin had split Adler's face. "Although, I'm sorry to hear you still can't get hold of your wife."

"Um," Fitzwilliam mumbled as he took a large gulp of coffee. He flipped open his laptop and went into the file he'd being using last night. "So I've split the items on the list into two groups. Things that, although would be nice to know, don't impact the accident itself."

"Like who was having an affair with whom?"

Fitzwilliam nodded. "And background information on Mrs Sterling and the earl that, ideally, I think we should be thorough on, but I accept isn't absolutely necessary to determine how the accident happened." He took another sip of coffee and set the cup down. "The other group is the stuff I think *could* have had a direct impact on the accident and therefore needs further investigation."

Adler cocked her head to one side. "And your reasoning is?"

"I can imagine a scenario where our lost foreign security detail in the black Range Rover, maybe not

paying attention or simply going too fast, encoun-
tered the earl, who we know was driving close to
the speed limit, yet frankly way too fast for a small
country lane in the dark. The earl swerved to avoid
a collision and came off the road. The Range Rover
carried on, probably in shock, then stopped just in
front of the junction. They then called the other two
guys in the estate car and told them what had happened. They met up, then both vehicles went back
to the scene, found the car, checked the passengers,
realised there was nothing they could do, searched
the boot to find ID but couldn't find anything. Then
maybe one of them recognised the earl. They pan-
icked when they realised they would be in big
trouble if anyone found out, so they legged it."

Adler pulled a face. "It's a great story, but what
do you have to support it in terms of evidence?"

"We have the open passenger door and the open
boot of the earl's car. We have the partly opened
case belonging to Gill. We also have the other footprints that could belong to two of the security guys,
and we have witness statements putting the two
vehicles in the area at the time of the accident. If
their timings are right, then it's likely they drove
past the accident scene."

"But them being in the area is not in dispute.

Reed said the drivers reported they were there, but they saw nothing," she pointed out.

"But we haven't seen those statements, have we? I think we need to examine them, then interview the drivers. We'll then get a feel for if they're lying or not. Plus clarity on the timing."

He closed his laptop cover and looked over at her. "What do you think?"

She leaned back in her chair and took a sip of her tea. "I think you have enough to raise it with Reed. But the scene of crime reports have nothing in them to support Mr and Mrs Maynard's statements about the passenger door or the boot being opened before they arrive on the scene. Similarly, the partly opened case could just be because Mrs Sterling packed in a hurry, and witnesses can be unreliable with timings. So be prepared that he might not think you have sufficient cause to keep the investigation open when they're under pressure to close it as soon as possible. Did you see in some newspapers this morning they're questioning why a date still hasn't been set for the funeral? The conspiracy theorists are having a field day. Any further delay is only going to increase their curiosity."

Fitzwilliam let out a deep sigh. *Do I really want to rock the boat?* Before he could contemplate any further, the door swung open, and Reed and Prior entered the room.

"My office, please, you two," Reed said as he walked past their desks.

"Morning," Prior said as he nodded, then followed Reed into his office.

Adler rose. "Your turn to make the drinks," she said as she picked up her pocketbook and her mug.

Blast! Why does it always seem to be my turn?

Thirty minutes later, an exhausted-looking Reed dropped the report he'd just read out loud to them onto his desk, rose and, moving in front of it, leaned back and crossed his arms. "Prior and I are happy with the report, but if either of you think we've missed anything, then say so now before we press the button and off it goes."

Fitzwilliam felt Adler's eyes on him and turned to look at her. She nodded her head.

"Fitzwilliam?" Reed caught his eye and raised an eyebrow.

Fitzwilliam cleared his throat. "I've asked for copies of the statements made by the security detail that got lost in the area on the night of the accident, sir, but I've been told by City they're not available.

Their systems say to refer to DCI Tim Street. Could you request them, sir, just so we can cross reference them to the witness statements, especially around timing?"

Reed continued to stare at him. "Why?" he asked curtly.

What does he mean, why? I've just told him. "Er, sorry, sir?"

"Why, Fitzwilliam? The men reported they saw nothing, so why do we need to cross-reference them to anything?"

"Well, sir. If our two witness statements are correct, then I don't know how they could have seen nothing. They must have driven past the accident site."

"Or they could've driven past right before it happened," Prior said as he stood up to stand next to Reed. "The estimated time of death carries on after they were spotted."

"But only by a few minutes, sir. If they are—"

Reed stood up. "The security detail has made a statement saying they saw nothing. Are you suggesting they're lying?"

Fitzwilliam hesitated. Reed and Prior were now both standing in front of the desk, facing him, their arms crossed. They looked like two bouncers outside an exclusive nightclub that he wasn't suitably dressed to enter. *I don't need to be a body language expert to work out they're not receptive to my theory...* But he still felt he needed to say it one last time before he accepted defeat. "It would be understandable if they were, sir. They must be worried about the consequences if they were in any way responsible for the earl being forced off the road."

The two men looked at each other, then Prior nodded to Reed, uncrossed his arms and mumbled, "I'll leave you to it. Ring me when you're done." With a brief glance at Fitzwilliam and Adler, he strode from the office.

What's going on? Fitzwilliam looked over at Adler. She gave a barely perceptible shrug.

Reed uncrossed his arms and moved round to sit behind his desk. He leaned forward and fixed them in his gaze. "What I'm going to say to you now is to go no further than this room. Do I make myself clear?"

What the?

Fitzwilliam and Adler nodded.

"Okay. Here's the thing. We have no proof the security detail was involved in the earl's accident. All we have are a couple of witness reports that state they saw vehicles that *look* like the ones who reported they were lost in the area. We have no number plates to link the sighting to the actual vehicles, and we have two statements by the occupants in those vehicles who say they saw nothing. So even if we *think* they may have been involved, there is nothing we can do to prove it—"

But the statements... Fitzwilliam opened his mouth, but Reed quickly raised his hands.

"I know you're going to say we need to see their statements and maybe even interview them." He shook his head. "That can't happen."

Fitzwilliam sagged back in his chair. *So they're going to just allow them to—*

"We cannot go to an important ally of this government and say, 'We think your security people have lied to the police about what they saw the night of the Earl of Rossex's death. In fact, we think they may have caused the accident themselves, then fled the scene, committing several criminal offences. We want to prove this, so we'd like you to hand them over to us so we can interview them. Is that okay with you? Oh, and by the way, witnesses cannot give number plates, although they think they *may* have been foreign ones, or a description of the passengers they saw as it was too dark, and it's possible that the accident happened *after* your guys were in the area as the estimated time of death goes beyond when they were spotted.'"

Well, when you put it like that...

Reed smiled wryly. "Look, Fitzwilliam, if I thought we had credible grounds to pursue this, then I wouldn't hesitate to stick my neck out. But can you imagine the political fallout, along with the diplomatic implications, and not to mention the re-action of the foreign press, if we accused another country of killing a member of the royal family, and then we can't prove it beyond reasonable doubt? Pointing fingers without evidence will cause too much of a strain on public relations."

Fitzwilliam nodded. He hadn't really thought about the investigation in those terms. He'd been in intelligence for several years, where they'd fre-quently raised concerns about the behaviour of other countries and their citizens, so he was more than aware of the political and diplomatic implica-tion of the information he was providing to his se-nior officers. However, it had not been part of his remit to deal with the potential fallout of those ac-cusations. That had been the job of those more se-nior to him. And now Reed was giving him a clear message: we cannot go down this route.

"Right. Well, as long as that's sorted, can we all agree the most likely scenario is the one Prior and I have laid out in our report, being that the earl was faced with an animal or a group of animals who ran out into the road or were possibly already standing in the car's path as it came around the corner, and the earl swerved to avoid it or them and thus lost control of his car that then led to the fatal crash. We have statements from several witnesses who confirm deer were active that evening in the area where the tragedy occurred, as well as animal markings and droppings the SOC officers took from the accident scene."

Fitzwilliam turned to look at Adler, and she nodded. "Yes, sir," they replied.

"Thank you. Prior and I will deliver our report at Gollingham Palace later this afternoon. I suggest you guys pack these offices up and then check out of your hotel and head back. Unless you hear otherwise from me, take tomorrow morning off to sort yourselves out at home, and I'll see you both in the office at GP in the afternoon."

"Yes, sir."

36

LATER AFTERNOON, SUNDAY 8 JANUARY

Fitzwilliam reached out to his mobile phone holder and cut the call on the screen. *Where is she?* He still hadn't heard from Amber, and he was getting worried. Had something happened to her? He'd have to swallow his pride and call her parents on their landline again.

While he waited for the call to connect, he turned on the car's heating. The afternoon sun was setting, and the temperature had dropped. It was going to be a long dark drive back to Surrey.

"Hello?"Amber's father's voice echoed around the car's interior.

"Ray, it's Richard. I'm trying to get hold of Amber but without success. Is she there?"

There was silence at the other end of the phone.

Where had he gone? Fitzwilliam's palms were suddenly clammy. *Is something wrong?*

"Richard?" Amber's mother came on the line, and his stomach dropped.

"What's wrong, Moira?"

"Nothing's wrong. You know what Ray's like on the phone."

Fitzwilliam's rapid heartbeat slowed down. He let out a sigh of relief. "I'm trying to get hold of Amber, but she's not answering her mobile."

"Silly girl left her charger here when she went off to the beach house. She borrowed someone's phone to let us know she was okay, so we wouldn't worry..."

She didn't ring me so I *wouldn't worry!*

"...and she's back tomorrow morning anyway. I'm sure she'll be in contact as soon as she's here and charges her phone back up."

So Amber was up at the beach house on her own without a phone. That didn't sound very safe. "But she's there on her own with no means to contact—"

"It's fine, Richard. She said she's met the neighbours, who are friendly, and she's perfectly safe. She told me she's enjoying having a break from everything."

From me, is probably what she means...

"I'll let her know you called as soon as she's back, all right?"

What more could he do? It wasn't his in-law's fault their daughter was being so unreasonable.

"Yes, of course, Moira. Thank you."

He ended the call and took a deep breath before letting it out slowly. His hopes that Amber would rush home when she found out he was on his way back from Fenshire and they could go out to dinner tonight and talk through whatever was bothering her were dashed. *I better stop and pick up something to eat on the way home...*

37

EARLY EVENING, SUNDAY 8 JANUARY

The lights grew brighter as Fitzwilliam reached the outskirts of London. He was glad he'd grabbed something to eat at the service station. He'd forgotten how much traffic there was on a Sunday night, with everyone returning to the capital after their weekend in the country. He knew it would be stop-start all the way home now. When he was about to switch on the radio, his mobile rang, startling him. Was it Amber? He glanced away from the road ahead and over to his phone screen. Withheld number. He shrugged and accepted the call.

"Fitzwilliam," he answered.

"Ah, Fitzwilliam." He sat up a little straighter when he recognised the voice of his boss. "Ma'am."

"So how did your little jaunt up to Fenshire

go?" Copson asked. "I hear we're waiting for the charge of treason to come through."

Blast! Who'd told his boss about that? Reed, no doubt. Probably at the same time as he'd asked her how quickly she could take her wayward sergeant back to Intelligence, never to have contact with the royal family again.

"I'm not sure I'm cut out for investigations, ma'am."

"Really?" She sounded surprised.

Surely that's what Reed would have told her.

"Because I've had a request for you to be transferred permanently to Reed's team."

"What?" Fitzwilliam couldn't stop himself from blurting out. "But how? Why? When?"

Copson laughed. "I don't know why you're so shocked. Reed was impressed with what he called your 'intrepid spirit'. He liked that you weren't daunted by dealing with the royal family face to face, and he thinks your tenacious and inquisitive nature will take you far."

Fitzwilliam closed his mouth. Could this be true? He'd assumed he'd become a bit of a thorn in Reed's side over the last week. Maybe he'd read the situation wrong? Maybe Reed liked to be challenged?

"Fitzwilliam?" Copson's voice had a touch of concern in it.

"Sorry, ma'am."

"So how do you feel about it? Do you want to stay with Investigations?"

"I don't know, ma'am. I didn't realise that option was on the table."

"Well, strictly, it wasn't. But I don't want to hold you back if you have a blossoming career there. Although, I have to warn you that even though you'll still be based at Gollingham Palace, you'll spend a lot more time travelling around the country. You'll also be working closely with the protection arm of PaIRS. Investigations has a much more proactive role than you might realise."

"Can I have some time to think about it, ma'am? I'd like to talk to Amber, see how she feels."

"Of course, take a few days. It's a great opportunity, Fitzwilliam, and Reed is keen to have you."

"Yes, ma'am."

"Okay, well, I'll leave you to your drive home. Pop in and see me later on in the week. If you have questions in the meantime, then give me a shout."

The line went dead. Fitzwilliam stared at the cars ahead of him in the queue of traffic merging onto the ring road and slowly shook his head. Would Amber be pleased he'd made such a good impression that Investigations wanted him permanently? Or would she be unhappy that the new role would take him away from home more frequently when she wanted them to spend time together? He shifted in his seat. Surely she could see it was a feather in his cap to be asked, and the move would speed up his chances of promotion? He sighed and moved the car into second gear as he accelerated onto the slip road. It would have to wait until tomorrow when she was back in communication…

38

MORNING, TUESDAY 10 JANUARY

"Fitzwilliam?"

Fitzwilliam jumped to his feet as Street's head appeared around the PaIRS' office door at Gollingham Palace.

"Sir." *What does he want? Is he looking for Reed?* "Reed isn't here, sir. He's—"

"I'm looking for you," Street replied as he walked in and closed the door.

Me?

"I hear they have offered you an opportunity to move permanently to Investigations. How do you feel about it?"

"Er, well, I'm very flattered, sir, and I'm seriously considering it." He just needed to talk to Amber, but after their brief and stilted conversation last night on the phone, he'd decided to wait until she was back tonight before he broached the subject. At least she couldn't slam the phone down on him if they were together in person!

"Well, for what it's worth, I think it would be a good move for you, sergeant."

"Thank you, sir. I appreciate your support."

"I also heard from Reed you have a theory about the earl's accident that unfortunately we weren't able to explore further because of a lack of concrete evidence and the risk of upsetting some important people." He walked across the room and lowered himself into Adler's chair opposite him. He indicated for Fitzwilliam to sit down. "Tell me about it."

"Really, sir? It's just an idea, and—"

"Yes, really. I'm interested." He leaned forward and, resting his elbows on the desk, raised his hands to his chin and nodded.

Twenty minutes later, when Fitzwilliam had explained his concerns and Street had asked some pertinent questions, they relapsed into silence.

Fitzwilliam studied the man on the other side of the desk to him. His eyes were looking down at the table as he slowly nodded. *What's he thinking? Does he think it's all a figment of my imagination?* Except, the questions he'd asked had been insightful and relevant. Fitzwilliam's stomach fluttered. *Does he think I'm onto something?*

"Well," the older man said as he looked up and caught Fitzwilliam's eye. "Reed and Prior have submitted their report, and we have adopted it as the official response. It will go to the coroner tomorrow. The inquest, when it happens in a few weeks' time, will probably reach a verdict of accidental death. As we speak right now, the Lord Chamberlain is agreeing on a date for the earl's ceremonial royal funeral with the king and queen. Nothing you or I do can change that. Do you understand?"

Suppressing a sigh, Fitzwilliam nodded. So had they sent Street to once again remind him that nothing could be done about his suspicions, and he should drop it? He bristled. *I don't need reminding it will cause too much trouble to pursue it any further.* But why had Street sat here listening to him and asking questions if it was all a pointless exercise?

"However."

There's a however?

"I think your scenario is not beyond the realm of possibility."

Fitzwilliam sat up straight.

Street raised his hand. "But before you get too excited, you need to realise nothing has changed. We cannot officially do anything about this. I can't share the full details of the statements the occupants of the Range Rover and the estate car made because you have insufficient security clearance, but I can tell you they state they saw nothing relevant during the time they were in the area. They also say they didn't get out of their vehicles. Their statements confirm they left the area at eleven-eighteen, only a few minutes out from your witnesses' statements."

So they might have been gone before the earl's accident after all. *But then why did Street just say my theory isn't beyond the realm of possibility?* "So you believe they're lying, sir?"

Street tilted his head to one side and frowned. "Just out of curiosity, why are you so keen to push this, Fitzwilliam?"

What should I say? That he didn't like the thought that someone had been responsible for the death of a young man in his prime and they'd probably get away with it? Or he felt Reed and Prior had predetermined the entire investigation from day one? He couldn't say that. "I don't like loose ends, sir."

Street nodded and smiled. "Me neither, Fitzwilliam."

So...?

"But we have no evidence to support the theory that these men caused or were at least in some way involved in the earl's accident. And after the uproar the appeal for the two vehicles caused, that ultimately led to a seemingly dead end, both the palace and my superiors have no appetite for what they see as wild theories. So whether or not I believe they are lying is irrelevant. There's nothing more you or I can do but accept that this is as far as it goes, I'm afraid." He rose.

He's right. There's no more to be done. "Okay, sir, thank you." Fitzwilliam jumped up.

Street headed to the door. As his hand rested on the handle, he turned.

"Of course, if you think of anything else or come across something you think may be relevant to this case, then please let me know."

Fitzwilliam nodded. "Yes, sir."

And with that, Street opened the door and disappeared outside.

Fitzwilliam let out a deep breath and sat down. He pinched his lips together and rubbed his forehead where a headache was beginning. He now needed to decide about if he wanted to move teams. Could he really ignore both Copson's and now Street's advice that moving to Investigations would be the right thing for his career? *Not really. I just have to convince Amber now.*

39

TWENTY MINUTES LATER, TUESDAY 10 JANUARY

"Hold my calls please, Susan," Street said to his personal assistant as he closed the door to the outer office and returned to his desk. He sat, then leaned down and pulled his briefcase onto his lap. He found the biometric fingerprint security panel and pressed his thumb on the small screen. *Beep, beep.* The case opened, and he unzipped an inside compartment, then withdrew a small pay-as-you-go phone.

Having returned the bag to the floor under his desk, he held his thumb against the side of the phone, depressing the small button there. A logo flashed up, followed by a passcode entry screen. He tapped in the eight-digit code and waited for the phone to unlock.

A message flashed up. *Do you need to talk to X?*

Street typed. *Yes*

The phone rang. Street pressed 'Accept call' and held the phone up to his left ear.

"Is it done?" The voice was Eastern European in origin.

"Yes," Street replied, leaning back in his chair.

"No loose ends?"

"No. They have accepted the security details' statements I have provided them with, and it's now considered a dead end. The inquest will return a verdict of accidental death."

"Good. Well, that's one less mess to deal with." There was a pause. "What about the letter? Why hasn't it been found yet?"

Street sat up and cleared his throat. "I don't know. I'm assured by my man on the ground that it was left as agreed, but it wasn't found in the earl's possessions."

"So where is it?"

"I don't think it matters. It was just a bit of added diversion. The press did a good enough job without it."

"Umm," the man huffed. "It's still messy."

"It's not important," Street emphasised. 'I have someone new who trusts me. I'll hear if anything crops up that needs to be dealt with. But I don't expect there to be anything.

Silence. Street resisted the urge to fill it. *I need to stay calm and in control.* He waited.

"So it's over then?"

"Yes," Street replied with purpose. "It's done."

"Okay." The call disconnected.

Street went into the phone's call history and deleted it, then pressed the button on the side again to switch the phone off. Returning it to his briefcase he stood up and let out a deep breath. *It's done. We've got away with it.*

40

EVENING, TUESDAY 10 JANUARY

Amber grabbed her wineglass from the dining table in their flat, and lifting it to her pinched lips, she took a gulp, her gaze never leaving her husband's.

Fitzwilliam looked away, his wife's steely stare unnerving him. This wasn't going how he'd planned. He'd assumed as it was their first evening together for two weeks that she would have mellowed after her week away by the beach and be pleased to see him. *Seems I've got it wrong on both counts.*

Amber pushed the plate of half-eaten chicken chow mien away from her and sighed. "I don't know why you're bothering to ask my opinion, Rich. It's clear you've already made up your mind." Her voice was slightly higher than normal. She began swilling around the red wine that remained in her glass as if she was about to do a wine tasting.

"I'm asking because I value your opinion, Amber." He tried not to sound stern. *But it really is like dealing with a petulant child sometimes.*

"So if I say I think it's a bad idea, then you'll stay where you are, will you?" She tilted her head to one side, her blonde feathered fringe falling over her left eye.

He frowned. *Is she just being antagonistic, or does she really think it's a bad idea?* "Do you think it's a bad idea then?"

She necked back the rest of her wine. "Does it matter what I think?"

He suppressed a groan. *Why can't she just answer the question?* "Yes. As I said, I value your opinion. I know it will mean I'm away a bit more than I am now, but both Copson and Street think it's a good move. You yourself said you thought I should have gone into Investigations when I first got the job at PaIRS, and I chose Intelligence, so—"

She slammed her empty wineglass down on the table, giving him a start. "Yes, and you didn't listen to me then. So why will you listen to me now?"

This time, he couldn't suppress the sigh that escaped his lips. *She clearly isn't in the mood to cooperate. I may as well give up and try again tomorrow.*

She jumped up. "Don't you sigh at me! I've been back for less than two hours, and all you've done is talk about your precious job. You haven't once asked me how I am or if I had a good break. It's all been about you!" She scooped up her empty glass, and waving it at him, she shouted, "You know what, Rich? I don't care if you take the job or not. Do what you want." Grabbing the half-full bottle of wine from the middle of the table, she stormed across the room, yelling, "I'm off to have a bath. Don't wait up for me!"

Fitzwilliam shook his head as he watched the back of his wife disappear around the door frame. *I give up!*

41

MORNING, MONDAY 30 JANUARY

"You know you don't have to be here if you don't want to, sis. I can handle it on my own. It's just a briefing from PaIRS about the inquest and what to expect." Fred looked with concern at his younger sister as he walked over to the window of the first floor sitting room where Bea was standing and touched her arm. "You should be resting."

"I'm all right, Fred. Really, I am. Now that Saturday is over and done with, this is the next hurdle to jump, and I need to deal with it." She patted his hand and smiled.

Not that she would be attending the inquest. Since her family had found out about her pregnancy, they'd been falling over themselves to protect her from any further upset. Even at James's funeral, which had taken place two days earlier, they had insisted she remained in the car until the last possible moment, when she'd then been escorted by her mother, sister, and mother-in-law into the hushed cathedral. In an unprecedented move, the four women had walked down the central aisle together, their arms intertwined in a show of support that had almost overwhelmed her. Meanwhile, following the coffin, her father the Duke of Arnwall, her brother Fred, her father-in-law the Earl of Durrland, her uncle the Prince of Wales, and her grandfather the king, had taken the brunt of the public's outpouring of grief, stoically remaining dignified as they'd slowly made their way past the estimated seventy thousand people who had taken to the streets to see the funeral procession wind its way along the streets of central London. Later that evening, her mother's private secretary had told Bea over a billion people from around the world had watched the royal funeral. She was glad she hadn't known that at the time.

But it was over now, and they just had the inquest to go. She'd already informed her grandfather she wouldn't be returning to royal duties any time in the foreseeable future. He'd reluctantly accepted her decision, although he'd told her mother he hoped once the pain lessened, she would reconsider.

But she wouldn't. All she wanted to do now was protect the precious part of James that remained and concentrate on raising his child.

There was a knock on the door, and Harris entered, followed by two men. *Oh no!* Her heart sank. *What's he doing here?*

"Detective Chief Inspector Reed and Detective Sergeant Fitzwilliam, your ladyship."

"Thank you, Harris," she said as Fred strolled across the room and held out his hand to each man in turn.

"Thank you for coming, gentlemen," Fred said as he steered them towards two large grey sofas opposite each other. "Please sit down."

Bea took a deep breath. *Come on, Bea. You can do this.* She moved to the seating area and joined the three men who had remained standing. Choosing an armchair between the sofas, she smiled and sat down. They followed suit.

Crossing her legs at the ankles, she darted a look at Fitzwilliam as Fred began talking.

He's plucky this sergeant. She had to give him that. After being asked to leave twice previously, she would have thought he wouldn't want to put himself in a position to be thrown out a third time. And yet here he was, sitting as upright as he could, encased in the rather squidgy sofa her father had fought so hard to keep against her mother's protestation it was too old and under-stuffed. He shifted forwards again, trying not to sink back in the corner. She suppressed a grin. It was good to see him squirm.

She turned her attention to the smaller man, who was currently telling Fred about what they could expect from the inquest. His smooth Scottish accent made her feel homesick for Drew Castle, her mother's family's private castle in Scotland. Her grandmother, the queen, had suggested she should go up there once the weather improved so she could rest and recover. On the other hand, her mother's best friend Lady Grace Bransgrove had asked Bea to join her and her daughter Sybil in Portugal for a month. *It will be warmer than Scotland!* Both options appealed to her, particularly because they would keep her out of the way of the press who remained camped outside Francis Court day and night even though it had been four weeks since James's accident.

She fiddled with the rings on her left hand.

Even when she'd left for London on Friday to prepare for the funeral the next day, as she'd been driven through the pack, her first venture outside the grounds since James's death, they had barraged her with questions, shouting so loudly she had heard them over the sound of the cameras.

Click, click, click.

"What was the relationship between the earl and Gill Sterling, my lady?"

"What was Mrs Sterling doing in your husband's car, countess?"

Click, click, click.

"Was your husband having an affair with Mrs Sterling, Lady Rossex?"

"Did you know, Lady Beatrice?"

On the eve of her husband's funeral. *Do they not have an ounce of compassion in their bones?*

She would dearly love to get away from the attention for a while. Maybe she would go to Portugal and hide there until things calmed down a bit. Assuming they ever would…

"So really, that's it," Reed said, smiling at Bea. *I hope Fred was listening!* She'd been zoning out more and more since James's death. No doubt a doctor would say she was hiding from reality. But to her, it just felt like the details of life didn't matter anymore. James was dead. Life's minutiae didn't interest her now. She returned Reed's smile and nodded.

"Unless there is anything new you'd like to tell us, Lady Rossex?" Fitzwilliam was now perched so precariously on the edge of the sofa his long legs were bunched underneath him like the smoking caterpillar in *Alice in Wonderland.*

She frowned. *What does he mean?*

"Unless something new has come to light or you have remembered anything you think we need to know?"

A shiver ran up her spine. *Is he implying I know something I haven't told them?* Her slightly swollen stomach dropped. She looked at his smug face, and for a moment, she thought she might get up and slap it. She clenched her hands together and rested them in her lap. *How dare he question my integrity!* If she knew something that was relevant, then of course she would've told them.

She met his gaze and, in her frostiest voice, said, "No, sergeant." He stared back, but when she didn't blink, he glanced away.

I bet he thinks I know what was going on between James and Gill, she seethed. But even though she'd told him twice now, he persisted in asking again. No one spoke to her like that. He was so disrespectful. *It's as if he cares nothing for the royal family and what we mean to the country.*

"Well, thank you, my lady, your lordship." Reed rose, smiling. "I'm sure it will all go smoothly."

A phone rang, and Fitzwilliam scrambled up,

thrusting his hand in his pocket to retrieve his mobile. He stared at the screen, then at Reed. "I need
to take this…"

*What? He's taking a call in the middle of a
meeting with us? How rude.*

She and Fred stood up.

Reed nodded, and Fitzwilliam mumbled, "I'm
so sorry," as he headed towards the door and let
himself out.

*Well, good riddance to him. I hope I will never
see him again. Ever!*

"I'm sorry, but we've been waiting for an urgent
call regarding that business with your aunt, so
please forgive Fitzwilliam for having to leave."

Bea's aunt on her mother's side, the Duchess of
Sulley, had had her laptop hacked two days before
and was beside herself with worry. *Well, I suppose
that* is *important.*

"Of course," Fred said.

But even so, Fitzwilliam was still judgemental
and didn't seem to approve of her or her family.
*What on earth is he doing in PaIRS anyway if he
feels that way?*

"My lady?" Reed looked at her enquiringly.
"Did you say something?"

"I was just wondering what DS Fitzwilliam is
doing in PaIRS when he so obviously disapproves

of us and our lifestyle. I can only conclude he's working from the inside to overthrow the monarchy."

Reed and her brother stared at her, open-mouthed.

Did I really say that out loud? Now Reed is going to think I'm unhinged and all because that awful man Fitzwilliam can't keep his mouth shut. I need to fix this... "I'm just teasing, chief inspector. Thank you so much for coming today." She held out her hand, and giving her an unsure smile, Reed shook it.

Harris appeared and showed him out. As the door closed, Fred turned to her. "What was that all about?"

42

LATE AFTERNOON, TUESDAY 7 FEBRUARY

The Society Page online article:

<u>Inquest into the Death of the Earl of Rossex Records Verdict</u>

The inquest into the death of James Wiltshire (24), the Earl of Rossex, was concluded today in central London when the coroner recorded a verdict of accidental death. Having already given permission to release the body of the earl a week ago so the ceremonial royal funeral could take place, the coroner concluded the earl lost control of his car while swerving to avoid something in the road, most likely an animal, that caused him to come off the road and plough his Audi RS4 into a tree. The earl was killed immediately, and his passenger Gill Sterling (27), the wife of the estate manager at Francis Court, died later in the hospital.

The inquest heard the earl was driving within the speed limit on the night of Tuesday, the third of January, and they found no alcohol or drugs in his blood system.

Lady Beatrice (21), the Countess of Rossex, did not attend her husband's inquest and has not been seen in public since his funeral ten days ago. A spokesperson for the countess said her ladyship and the earl's parents the Earl and Countess of Durrland were satisfied with the verdict of accidental death and requested now that the inquest is over, they be left alone to come to terms with their loss.

43

NINE YEARS LATER...

Detective Inspector Richard Fitzwilliam of the Protection and Investigation (Royal) Services sighed as he picked up the paper opener from his desk and studied the back of the envelope in front of him. There was no getting away from it. This was it. The final nail in the coffin of his marriage. He slit it open and took out the contents. The thin brown-grey paper felt flimsy in his hand. The decree absolute. The final certificate confirming that he and Amber were no longer married. He raised his hand to his heart, where an ache took his breath away for a second.

There were many things Fitzwilliam was proud of in his life — his distinguished Army career, his part in protecting his sister from their errant father and flaky mother, his promotion to inspector three years ago (making him one of the youngest inspectors in PaIRS), his uncluttered and stylish flat. But the failure of his marriage wasn't one of them. And as easy as it would have been to solely blame Amber —after all, she'd been the one who'd had an affair with an old school flame, who she was now living with in Spain where they ran a bar and restaurant on the Costa Del Sol— he knew deep down that he had to bear some element of responsibility for their relationship's breakdown. *How did I get it so wrong?* he mused, not for the first time in the last seven years since Amber had told him their marriage was over and she was leaving him to be with someone else. He acknowledged now that he'd buried his head in the sand for a long time, ignoring their lack of communication, optimistically assuming they would get back on track once he wasn't so busy with work. But of course, he had always been busy with work.

He sighed as he put down the paper that signalled the end of the process he had been so reluctant to start. At least Amber would be happy now. She could marry her beach-bum and live happily ever after. Whereas him…

The ringing of a phone startled him, and he grabbed the phone on his office desk. "Hello?"

"Inspector Fitzwilliam?" a woman's voice asked.

"Yes."

"I'm ringing from the office of Superintendent Street. Are you available to come and see him now?"

"Yes, of course. I'll be there shortly."

"Thank you. It's room three hundred and thirty in security block two."

He put the handset back on its cradle and rose, grabbing his jacket from the back of his chair. *I wonder what Street wants?* He'd seen little of the former chief inspector since they'd promoted Street six months ago.

Fifteen minutes later, he stepped into the outer office of room three hundred and thirty and approached the desk, where a dark-haired woman typed furiously. She looked up as he stopped just short of her desk. "DI Fitzwilliam?"

He nodded.

"The superintendent is expecting you. Please go right in." She indicated the office behind her where Fitzwilliam could see Street leaning back in his office chair, reading a piece of paper. "Can I get you a tea or coffee, inspector?"

He shook his head. "No, thank you. I'm trying to cut down."

She smiled and nodded as he walked past her and entered the office. Street jumped up and walked towards him, smiling. "Ah, Fitzwilliam, it's been a while." He held out his hand, and Fitzwilliam shook it.

"Yes, sir. And congratulations on your promotion."

"Thank you. Please take a seat."

Street returned to his desk while Fitzwilliam lowered himself into the chair opposite him.

"Something unexpected has come up, and I need your help."

Fitzwilliam leaned forward. *This could be interesting...*

"When you were investigating the Earl of Rossex's death, do you remember that the City Police recovered the earl's overnight bag from his apartment in Knightsbridge Court and sent it to Fenshire CID to inspect?"

Fitzwilliam shrugged. "Vaguely, sir. I don't recall there being anything of any interest in there."

Street nodded. "Quite so. They returned the contents to Lady Rossex a few days later."

Fitzwilliam frowned. *Where is this going?*

"Except, for some reason, they didn't return the bag itself. Instead, they marked it up as evidence and eventually put it into storage at Fenshire Headquarters. Recently, they relocated the contents of the warehouse to a larger facility, and to cut a long story short, when moving the earl's bag, a letter dropped out."

Fitzwilliam's eyes widened. *A letter?*

Street opened his drawer and took out a piece of A4 paper with a photocopy of an envelope on it. He placed it on the table. "It was, presumably, caught in the bag's lining."

Fitzwilliam leaned in even closer. On the front of the envelope was one word — Bea.

"Is it from the earl?" Fitzwilliam asked, leaning back.

"Yes. According to the handwriting experts at Fenshire CID, it's the Earl of Rossex's handwriting."

Fitzwilliam looked at the photo again. *What does it say inside? Will it throw any more light on what happened nine years ago? Does it reveal what the earl was going to tell his MI6 contact? Why is Street telling me?* He looked up at the superintendent.

"This must be handled carefully, Fitzwilliam. We need to know if the contents of the letter have any material impact on the inquest's verdict of accidental death. However, it's addressed to Lady Rossex, and therefore, we cannot simply open it. And of course, we also need to be very discreet If this letter got into the public domain, whatever it says, it could be explosive."

Fitzwilliam nodded. Even nine years after the earl's accident, the press still seemed to shoehorn speculation about why Gill Sterling had been in the earl's car into articles written about anyone in Princess Helen's family. And even though Lady Rossex had kept herself quietly hidden, raising her and her late husband's son Samuel at Francis Court, every time she ventured out for a royal family event, the papers, led by *The Daily Post*, would re-hash the whole incident again. Yes, he could only imagine what it would be like if a letter from the earl to his wife got into the hands of the press.

Street continued, "It's the reason I left it with CID in Fenshire and didn't risk moving it here. The fewer people who have eyes on it, the better."

Still wondering what it had to do with him, Fitzwilliam nodded again.

"So, Fitzwilliam, I want you to go to Fenshire and collect the letter from CID. While you're there, I've arranged for the handwriting experts to give you a quick lesson on how to spot if the letter inside is a fake."

A fake? "Is that likely, sir?"

Street shook his head. "I don't think so, but we

need to be cautious. This letter has suddenly turned up out of the blue. It's possible, although unlikely, that someone has planted it maliciously. Then I want you..."

Fitzwilliam's heart beat faster. *He not going to ask me to—*

"...to take the letter to Lady Rossex and hand it to her in person. You will need to explain the situation and ask her for permission to read it. Afterwards, I want you to report back to me on the contents."

You have to be kidding! Me? "But sir, my previous encounters with her ladyship have been, shall we say, strained, so I don't know if—"

"I'm aware of your history with Lady Rossex. However, not only do I think your diplomatic skills have improved considerably since then—" He gave Fitzwilliam a wry smile. "But also it has to be someone who is familiar with the case and who her ladyship knows. Reed would have been the obvious choice, of course, but with his wife's recent ill health..." He trailed off. DCI Angus Reed's wife was currently ongoing a course of chemotherapy, and although they hoped she would make a full recovery, Reed had taken a leave of absence to look after her while she underwent treatment.

"So that leaves you as the next best option."

Fitzwilliam's mind turned over. He most definitely did *not* want to see the aloof Lady Rossex and have to tell her a letter from her husband written nine years ago had only just come to light and now he needed to know what it said. He cringed. *That won't be a pleasant conversation. Who knows how she'll react?* Would he be asked to leave again? To be asked to leave once could be considered unfortunate. To be asked to leave twice could be considered unlucky. But to be asked to leave a third time…

But then he couldn't deny he was more than a little curious to know what was in the letter and if it would help answer some questions they hadn't been able to answer at the time of the investigation.

"Okay, sir."

"Great," Street said as he rose and held out his hand to Fitzwilliam.

Jumping up, Fitzwilliam took it and returned the firm handshake.

"I'll let Fenshire CID know to expect you later today."

"Yes, sir."

Fitzwilliam headed to the door.

"Oh, and Fitzwilliam?"

He turned. "Yes, sir."

"Try not to get thrown out a third time."

My sweet Bea,

There is no easy way to tell you this. I'm sorry, but I'm leaving.

I know it will sound like a cliché, but please believe me when I say it's not you, it's me.

I will always love you, Bea. You have been my smart, beautiful, and funny best friend ever since we were children. But I'm not in love with you and I'm not sure I ever have been. And if you're honest with yourself, I think you'll realise that you have never been in love with me either.

Since we were adults, we've always focused our relationship on our public life — that string of activities and duties to perform has come first. You accept your life of duty. You accept the responsibility that comes with privilege. And even though you hate being the centre of attention, you put on a smile and face the press when you know it's required. But I'm not like you, Bea.

Deep down, I have always wanted more. The last twenty-five years of doing what everyone expected of me has meant there is almost no me left any more. The right school, the right university, the right job, the right wife - I have tried to live up to the mantle of the future Earl of Durrland. But time *and time again I have fallen short and now I'm exhausted. I can no longer see what value I have to you, the royal family, or my parents. No one asks my advice or wants my contribution, no one needs me, Bea. Not even you.*

On top of feeling like a spare part, the constant attention from the press every time we step out of Francis Court has become unbearable for me. I've said nothing until now because I didn't want you to think I wasn't able to stick out my stiff upper lip and suck it up, like you do. But the truth is, I can't.

I don't know how long I could have carried on like this, but four months ago, something happened that changed everything for me — I met Gill Sterling.

We were just friends to start, meeting up for coffee and walking in the grounds together, two 'extras' at Francis Court, blending into the background while all eyes were on the major stars. We talked about our lives and how we both felt trapped and unhappy. It was such a relief to talk to someone who understood. Before I was aware of what was happening, I fell in love. It was earth-shattering, all-consuming love. Something I had accepted I would never experience.

Although reluctant at first, she eventually told me Alex had been abusing her for years. Recently, it had become more physical. I have seen the marks on her face, her wrists and her legs. She was at her wits' end. She was frightened if she said anything that Alex would punish her. Since then, all I have wanted to do is take Gill somewhere safe, away from the husband who hurts her. It's taken a while to persuade her to trust me, but Alex has been getting more and more controlling recently and she has finally agreed to let me help. We are off to Mexico and then who knows? We will find the right place for us to settle down. Somewhere we can be our true selves.

I'm so sorry, Bea, but I can't face telling you in person. I expect the press will go crazy about this and I will do anything I can to help mitigate the inevitable scrutiny, so you have my permission to tell them whatever you need to. The family will know how to handle it. Let me know what is going to be said and I will issue a statement of confirmation. Of course, I must eventually tell my parents I have left. They will be enormously disappointed in me, but then what's new?

Gill will tell Alex she's going back to live with her family in Ireland, and she wants a divorce. She will warn him if he tries to find her, she will go to the press. I doubt Alex will say anything in the circumstances.

No one need know we are going away together.
I leave tomorrow morning and she is flying to join
me a few days later. There is no reason why anyone
will make the connection.

I hope one day you will forgive me. For once in
my life, I must do what is right for me.

Your loving,

James x

I hope you enjoyed *An Early Death*. If you did then please consider letting other know by writing a short review on Amazon or Goodreads, or even both. Thank you.

Will everything go to plan at Drew Castle? Not likely! Read the next book in the A Right Royal Cozy Investigation series *A Dead Herring*. You can order it on Amazon or where you buy your paperback.

Want to know how Bea and Perry solved their first crime together without knowing it? Then join my readers' club and receive a FREE novella,

A Toast To Trouble at https://www.subscribepage. com/helengoldenauthor_bmatttrm or if you'd prefer you can buy the ebook or paperback in the Amazon store.

For other books by me, take a look at the back pages.

If you want to find out more about what I'm up to you can find me on Facebook at *helengoldenauthor* or on Instagram at *helengolden_author*.

Be the first to know when my next book is available. Follow Helen Golden on Amazon, Book-Bub, and Goodreads to get alerts whenever I have a new release, preorder, or a discount on any of my books.

CHARACTERS IN ORDER OF APPEARANCE
AN EARLY DEATH

James Wiltshire — The Earl of Rossex and heir to the Earldom of Durrland. Lady Beatrice's husband.

Lady Beatrice — The Countess of Rossex. Daughter of Charles Astley, the Duke of Arnwall and Her Royal Highness Princess Helen. Granddaughter of the current king.

Gill Sterling — the wife of Francis Court's estate manager.

Alex Sterling — Francis Court's estate manager.

Richard Fitzwilliam — detective sergeant at *PaIRS (Protection and Investigation (Royal) Service)* an organisation that provides protection and security to the royal family and who investigate any threats against them. *PaIRS* is a division of *City Police*, a police organisation based in the capital, London.

Amber Fitzwilliam — Richard Fitzwilliam's wife.

Penny — Black Labrador, given to James Wiltshire as a puppy.

Rory Glover — The Earl and Countess of Rossex's private secretary.

Mr & Mrs Fraser — Butler/handyman/driver and cook/housekeeper.

Hayden Saunders — Works in investigations team in PaIRS. Currently away on leave climbing a mountain in Mexico.

Freddie Stamp — Works in Intelligence in PaIRS with Fitzwilliam.

Dave — Old school friend of Amber Fitzwilliam's.

Lady Sarah Rosdale — Lady Beatrice's elder sister. Twin of Fred Astley. Managers events at Francis Court.

Characters In Order Of Appearance

Earl and Countess of Durrland — James Wiltshire's parents William and Joan Wiltshire.

Charles Astley — Duke of Arnwall. Lady Beatrice's father.

HRH Princess Helen — Duchess of Arnwall. Mother of Lady Beatrice. Daughter of the current king.

Robert (Robbie) Rosdale — Lady Sarah's newly born son.

John Rosdale — Lady Sarah's husband.

King Henry & Queen Mary - current British king and his wife. Lady Beatrice's maternal grandparents.

Frederick (Fred) Astley — Earl of Tilling. Lady Beatrice's elder brother and twin of Lady Sarah Rosdale. Ex-Intelligence Army Officer. Future Duke of Arnwall.

Dawn Fitzwilliam — Richard and Elise Fitzwilliam's mother.

Desperate Dougie - Dawn Fitzwilliam's partner.

Elise Fitzwilliam — Richard Fitzwilliam's sister.

Rhys Boyce — Elise's fiancé and Richard Fitzwilliam's future brother-in-law.

Naomi — Princess Helen's maid.

Tim & Kim Maynard — local couple who come across the account scene.

Frances Copson — detective chief inspector in PaIRS Intelligence, Richard Fitzwilliam's boss

Brian Goody - principle private secretary to King Henry

Angus Reed — detective chief inspector, investigations team PaIRS, Richard Fitzwilliam's temporary boss.

Emma Adler — detective sergeant, investigations team PaIRS.

Matt Prior — detective chief inspector, Fenshire CID.

Simon Lattimore — detective constable, Fenshire CID.

Roisin — Simon Lattimore's housemate who works in Forensics at Fenshire Police.

Sharron Franks — Simon Lattimore's fiancee, teacher.

Paul Turner — detective sergeant, Fenshire CID.

Moria and Ray Lawler — Amber's parents, Richard Fitzwilliam's in-laws.

Characters In Order Of Appearance

Perry Juke — tour guide at Francis Court.

Ellie Gunn — Francis Court's shift supervisor in the cafe.

Claire Beck — friend of Perry Juke. Works in Human Resources at Francis Court.

Mrs C — Sophie Crammond, housekeeper at Francis Court.

Tim Street — detective chief inspector, currently on secondment from PaIRS to MI6

Harris/Mr Harris — butler at Francis Court and valet to Charles Astley, the Duke of Arnwall.

A BIG THANK YOU TO...

I continue to be amazed at the support my friends and family are giving me as I move along this journey of being an author. This being the fifth book I've written (including my free novelette *Tick, Tock, Mystery Clock*) I had expected everyone but me to be less excited each time I published a book, but that hasn't been the case. A big thank you to you all for your enduring encouragement and interest.

To my parents Ann and Ray, who are with me through every step of the process, from beta reading to final eyes. Your support is invaluable.

To my beta readers Lis and Lesley, thank you for your insightful and constructive feedback.

To my editor Marina Grout, you continue to help me improve as a writer and I'm so glad to have you in my corner.

To my lovely friend Carolyn Bruce for being

that critical additional set of eyes for me before publication.

And last, but most definitely not least, to you, my readers. Thank you for your generous reviews and feedback in the series so far. I love that you love my characters as much as I do. Please continue to get in touch, I'm always keen to hear from you. There is more coming from Lady Beatrice, Daisy, Perry, Simon, and Fitzwilliam, and I hope we can carry on enjoying spending time with them, together.

As always I may have taken a little dramatic license when it comes to police procedures, so any mistakes or misinterpretations, unintentional or otherwise, are my own.

ALSO BY HELEN GOLDEN

A novella lenght prequal in the series A Right Royal Cozy investiation series. With Perry and Bea working against each other, can they still save the party—or will it be ruined beyond repair along with Francis Court's reputation as a gold-standard venue?

A short prequal in the series A Right Royal Cozy Investigation. Can Perry Juke and Simon Lattimore work together to solve the mystery of the missing clock before the thief disappears? FREE novelette when you sign up to my readers' club. See end of final chapter for details. Ebook only.

First book in the A Right Royal Cozy Investigation series. Amateur sleuth, Lady Beatrice, must pit her wits against Detective Chief Inspector Richard Fitzwilliam to prove her sister innocent of murder. With the help of her clever dog, her flamboyant co-interior designer and his ex-police partner, can she find the killer before him, or will she make a fool of herself?

Second book in the A Right Royal Cozy Investigation series. Amateur sleuth, Lady Beatrice, must once again go up against DCI Fitzwilliam to find a killer. With the help of Daisy, her clever companion, and her two best friends, Perry and Simon, can she catch the culprit before her childhood friend's wedding is ruined? Also in Audio format.

The third book in the A Right Royal Cozy Investigation series. When DCI Richard Fitzwilliam gets it into his head that Lady Beatrice's new beau Seb is guilty of murder, can the amateur sleuth, along with the help of Daisy, her clever westie, and her best friends Perry and Simon, find the real killer before Fitzwilliam goes ahead and arrests Seb? Also in Audio format.

When the dead body of the event's planner is found at the staff ball that Lady Beatrice is hosting at Francis Court, the amateur sleuth, with help from her clever dog Daisy and best friend Perry, must catch the killer before the partygoers find out and New Year's Eve is ruined.

A DEAD HERRING

Snow descends on Drew Castle in Scotland cutting the castle off and forcing Lady Beatrice along with Daisy her clever dog, and her best friends Perry and Simon to cooperate with boorish DCI Fitzwilliam to catch a killer before they strike again.

I SPY WITH MY LITTLE DIE

A murder at Gollingham Palace sparks a hunt to find the killer. For once, Lady Beatrice is happy to let DCI Richard Fitzwilliam get on with it. But when information comes to light that indicates it could be linked to her husband's car accident fifteen years ago, she is compelled to get involved. Will she finally find out the truth behind James's tragic death?

A COCKTAIL TO DIE FOR

An unforgettable bachelor weekend for Perry filled with luxury, laughter, and an unexpected death.
Can Bea, Perry, and his hen's catch the killer before the weekend is over?

DYING TO BAKE

Bake Off Wars is being filmed on site at Francis Court and everyone is buzzing. But when much-loved pastry chef and judge, Vera Bolt, is found dead on set, can Bea, with the help of her best friend Perry, his husband Simon, and her cute little terrier, Daisy, expose the killer before the show is over?

A DEATH OF FRESH AIR

Even in a charming seaside town, secrets don't stay buried for long as Bea and Perry discover when they uncover the remains of a chef who disappeared 3 years ago. As they unravel a web of professional rivalries and buried grudges, they must race against time to solve the murder before the grand opening of Simon's new restaurant.

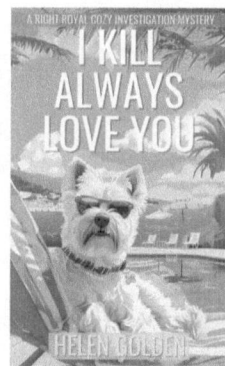

I KILL ALWAYS LOVE YOU

Lady Beatrice's peaceful holiday in Portugal is shattered when a Hollywood star's husband is found dead. What appears to be an accident soon reveals itself as murder. Tasked with clearing an innocent woman's name, Bea and Rich must untangle a web of lies to uncover the truth before it's too late.

PAPERBACKS AVAILABLE FROM WHEREVER YOU BUY YOUR BOOKS.

www.ingramcontent.com/pod-product-compliance
Lightning Source LLC
Chambersburg PA
CBHW050547190726
48283CB00007B/2041